The Algorithm

AI Dating Gone Wrong

C. P. RAMCHANDANI

The Algorithm (AI Dating Gone Wrong)

Published by Midas Publications

ISBN: 978-93-5655-082-7

For anyone who's ever been told they're "incompatible"— and chose to build something beautiful anyway.

And for those still searching: sometimes the best matches are the ones that don't make sense on paper.

The Algoritm

Contents

1. The Algorithm

Maya

The thing about jumping off a cliff is that you have to commit.

Not metaphorically—though Maya had done plenty of that too—but literally, right now, with her phone in one hand and the GoPro in the other, standing at the edge of a limestone outcropping in Thailand while her tour guide shouted instructions in Thai-inflected English she was only half-processing.

"On three! One, two—"

Maya jumped on two. She always jumped on two.

The camera caught everything: the moment of weightlessness, her scream morphing into laughter, the turquoise water rushing up to meet her, the explosion of white bubbles and muffled chaos.

When she surfaced, gasping and grinning, her first thought wasn't that it was incredible or I'm alive but rather: that's going to get at least 50K views.

She was right. By the time she'd toweled off and checked her phone, the video had already hit 47K, comments flooding in:

@adventureawaits: QUEEN BEHAVIOR

@travelwithTom: How do you just DO that???

@maya_superfan_01: Marry me

Maya screenshotted that last one to send to Suzie with three crying-laughing emojis.

Suzie's response came immediately: You know this is avoidance behavior, right?

Maya stared at the message, smile fading slightly. Her thumb hovered over the keyboard. She could defend herself—she was working, this was her job, she'd jumped off cliffs in seven different countries and it had never been about avoidance before—but instead she just sent back: Love you too bestie with a heart emoji.

That was four days ago.

Now she was back in Mountain View, jet-lagged and vaguely cranky, standing in the kitchen of the house she shared with Suzie and their other roommate, Carlos (software engineer, almost never home). The kitchen was chaos: Carlos's protein shake containers in the sink, Suzie's wedding photography contracts spread across the counter, Maya's passport and rumpled receipts scattered between them.

"You have taxes due in three weeks," Suzie said, not looking up from her laptop.

Maya was trying to remember which drawer held the regular coffee and which held the emergency espresso. "I'll figure it out."

"You said that last quarter."

"And I figured it out."

"You paid a penalty."

"A small penalty." Maya found the coffee, began scooping it with more force than necessary. "Are we really doing this at—" she checked her phone, "—seven in the morning?"

"It's noon. You're still in Bangkok time." Suzie finally looked up, her pixie cut somehow perfect despite the early hour. She had that expression, the one that meant she was about to say something Maya didn't want to hear. "Also, this came for you."

She slid a heavy cream-colored envelope across the counter.

Maya stared at it. "What is that?"

"Open it."

Maya picked it up like it might bite. Inside was a card—expensive cardstock, the kind that felt rich—with embossed text:

> *You've been selected for exclusive early access to SYNAPSE:*
> *Silicon Valley's most advanced AI-powered connection platform.*
> *94% success rate. Zero guesswork.*
> *Stop swiping. Start syncing.*

Below that, a QR code and an activation code.

Maya looked up. "You entered me in a dating app contest."

"I won it at a wedding expo. Thought you could use it."

"I don't use dating apps."

"Exactly." Suzie closed her laptop with a decisive click. "May, you're twenty-seven. You haven't been in a relationship longer than three months since college. You live out of a carry-on. Your last five Instagram posts have been from five different countries—"

"Six," Maya corrected. "I stopped in Taipei."

"—and every time I ask if you're happy, you show me engagement metrics." Suzie's voice softened. "I'm worried you're collecting experiences instead of actually having them."

The coffee maker gurgled aggressively, filling the silence.

Maya ran her thumb over the embossed lettering. "This is a six-month waitlist app. People pay like, thousands of dollars for this."

"It's free for contest winners. One year, fully activated." Suzie stood, gathering her contracts. "Look, I'm not saying you need to find a husband tomorrow. But maybe just... try? Let an algorithm do the work for once. See what happens."

She left before Maya could argue.

Maya stared at the card, then at her phone, still showing the Thailand cliff jump video. The comments had climbed to 89K. Someone had added: Imagine being this free.

She took a photo of the Synapse card, captioned it: *My bestie thinks I need an AI to fix my life. Should I let a robot play matchmaker? Vote in stories.*

The poll went up. Within minutes: 67% YES, 33% NO.

Maya looked at the activation code again. Then, before she could overthink it—because overthinking was how you ended up not jumping—she scanned the QR code.

Derek

The problem with routine was that it made anomalies obvious.

Derek noticed the email at 6:47 AM, exactly three minutes after his alarm, while he was lacing his running shoes in the precise order he'd been using for four years: left shoe, right shoe, double knot on both, check tightness. The email was nestled between his morning news digest and a calendar reminder about his 8:30 AM meeting.

> *Subject: SYNAPSE MATCH INCOMING - Prepare for Profile Activation*

He stared at it while his coffee cooled in its designated spot on his kitchen counter (right side, three inches from the edge, coaster underneath).

He hadn't signed up for Synapse.

Derek unlaced his shoes, opened his laptop, and methodically began checking: email filters (nothing), recent logins (only his), security settings (unchanged). His cursor hovered over the email. Spam? Phishing? Some elaborate scheme that would—

His phone rang. Marcus.

"Did you do this?" Derek answered.

"Good morning to you too, bro." Marcus's voice was muffled, probably still in bed. "Did I do what at seven in the morning?"

"Sign me up for a dating app."

A pause. Then: "Oh shit, it worked?"

Derek closed his eyes. "Marcus."

"Okay, listen—" Derek could hear Marcus sitting up, springs creaking. "James and I thought you needed help. You've been single for a year, you turned down three setups, and last week you told me your evening plans were 'reorganizing your spice cabinet alphabetically.' Not by cuisine. Alphabetically."

"It's more efficient."

"It's depressing, man." Marcus's voice gentled. "Look, James won a couples' access code at some Meta event. You can't use Synapse alone—it's designed for simultaneous matching. He gave me his plus-one code. I used it for you. The algorithm does everything. You literally just have to show up."

Derek looked at his running shoes, still unlaced. His schedule was now off by four minutes. "I don't have time for this."

"You have a color-coded calendar with thirty-minute blocks labeled 'flex time.' You have time."

"That flex time is for—"

"Being flexible. I know. Use it for this." Marcus paused. "Elena's engaged, by the way. Saw it on Instagram last night. That guy from her London office."

Derek's hand tightened on the phone. "Good for her."

"Is it though?"

"Yes." Derek's voice came out firmer than he felt. "She deserves to be happy."

"So do you." A beat. "Just try it. Three months. If it doesn't work, I'll stop bothering you about your love life until you're forty. Deal?"

Derek looked at the email again, then at his meticulously organized apartment: books arranged by subject then author, kitchen spotless, everything in its place. The life he'd built. Stable. Predictable.

Safe.

"Fine," he heard himself say. "Three months."

"Yes! Okay, so you'll need to complete the profile questionnaire—it's long, like three hundred questions—"

"Three hundred?"

"It's an algorithm, bro. It needs data. Just answer honestly. The app will handle the rest." Marcus's grin was audible. "Trust me, this is gonna be good."

After they hung up, Derek sat at his kitchen table with his laptop and opened the questionnaire. The first question appeared:

On a scale of 1-10, how comfortable are you with spontaneity?

Derek clicked 2.

Three days later, Derek had completed all 347 questions (Marcus had undercounted). He'd answered them methodically, during his designated "personal admin" time slots: 45 minutes after dinner Tuesday, 30 minutes Wednesday morning, the final session Thursday evening.

The app had asked everything: How do you handle conflict? What's your ideal Saturday? Do you prefer planning or improvising? How important is financial stability? What does commitment mean to you?

Derek had been honest, sometimes painfully so.

Question 187: Describe your perfect partner in three words.

He'd typed: Stable. Compatible. Present.

Then he'd stared at it for five minutes before adding a fourth word: Unexpected.

He deleted it immediately.

Now, Friday morning, 6:47 AM, his phone lit up with a notification:

SYNAPSE MATCH FOUND
Compatibility Score: 97.8%
Click to view profile

Derek, mid-run on his usual route through Shoreline Park, stopped. His heart rate monitor showed an unusual spike. He told himself it was from the run.

He clicked.

The profile loaded: a photo of a woman mid-laugh, hair whipping around her face, some tropical location behind her. She was beautiful in a way that made him nervous—the kind of beautiful that suggested chaos and adventure and everything Derek had spent his adult life organizing against.

Maya Reyes, 27
Travel Content Creator
"Life's too short for itineraries."

Derek scrolled through her profile pictures: cliff jumping, street food markets, festivals with crowds he'd find overwhelming, a selfie at airport security with the caption Home is wherever my carry-on lands.

His phone buzzed again:

FIRST SYNC SESSION MANDATORY
Location: Red Rock Coffee - Castro Street
Tomorrow, 10:00 AM
Failure to attend will result in match expiration

Derek looked at his calendar. Tomorrow was Saturday. He had: 6 AM run, 7:30 breakfast, 8:00-9:30 meal prep, 10:00-11:00 flex time, 11:00 grocery shopping...

He could move grocery shopping.

He could make this work.

He had to make this work because Marcus would never let him hear the end of it if he didn't, and also because—

He looked at Maya's profile again. At that laugh caught mid-motion. At the way she seemed so impossibly free.

—because Elena had called him boring. Predictable. Had said she felt like she was dating a spreadsheet.

Maybe the algorithm knew something he didn't.

Derek modified his calendar, sent Marcus a text (I have a match), and finished his run exactly 6.2 miles, same as always.

He didn't notice he'd been running faster until he checked his watch.

Maya

"This is a disaster," Maya said, staring at her phone.

"Let me see." Suzie leaned over from the driver's seat.

They were parked outside Red Rock Coffee, ten minutes early (Maya had been aiming for fashionably late, but Suzie had driven and refused to enable her). Through the window, Maya could see the café was moderately crowded—tech workers on laptops, morning coffee crowd, a few couples.

She pulled up Derek's profile again.

"Oh," Suzie said. "Oh no."

"Right?"

"He's..."

"Hot but terrifying," Maya finished. "Look at his bio: 'Seeking meaningful connection built on shared values and long-term compatibility.' Who talks like that?"

"Someone serious about relationships?"

"Someone who's going to judge my entire life." Maya scrolled through his pictures. Unlike her chaotic travel photos, his were carefully curated: a professional headshot, hiking (on a marked trail, of course), at some tech conference, one photo at what looked like a family dinner. Everyone looked happy and composed.

Maya's last family dinner photo involved her dad accidentally setting the tablecloth on fire.

"His hobbies are 'running, reading, cooking, and strategic board games.'" Maya looked up. "Strategic. Board games."

"You like Monopoly."

"I like winning at Monopoly by creating housing shortages and making everyone cry. That's different." Maya slumped in her seat. "We're 97.8% compatible. How? How is that mathematically possible? Look at him. Look at me."

Suzie studied both profiles. "You're both attractive."

"Not helpful."

"You both clearly care about your work."

"He works in finance. I jump off things for a living."

"Maybe that's the point." Suzie turned to face her fully. "May, you know I love you. But you date guys who are exactly like you—spontaneous, travel-obsessed, commitment-phobic. And they all end the same way: fun for two months, then someone gets on a plane and that's it."

Maya's fingers found her compass necklace. "So you think I should date someone boring?"

"I think you should date someone who might actually stay."

Through the café window, Maya spotted him: Derek Chen, arriving exactly on time, pausing to hold the door for someone, scanning the interior with careful precision. He looked... exactly like his photos. Put-together. Controlled. Like someone who'd never missed a deadline or forgotten where he parked.

"I can't do this," Maya said.

"Yes you can."

"What if he hates me?"

"Then you'll have great content about how AI dating is a scam." Suzie gently pushed her shoulder. "Go. Jump on two."

Maya took a breath, checked her lipstick in the mirror, and got out of the car before she could overthink it.

She was doing this.

She was absolutely doing this.

She was going to prove the algorithm wrong, document the whole disaster, and get incredible engagement in the process.

She pulled open the café door.

Derek Chen turned, making eye contact.

Maya's first thought was: Oh no, he's more attractive in person.

Her second thought was: We are going to be a complete disaster.

She smiled anyway.

"Hi," she said. "I'm Maya. You must be my 97.8% compatible nightmare."

***

2. Coffee and Contradictions

Derek

Derek had arrived seven minutes early, which gave him time to secure a table with optimal positioning: back corner, away from the bathroom and kitchen traffic, two chairs angled for conversation but not so close as to feel invasive. He'd ordered his usual—medium dark roast, no sugar, no cream—and was reviewing his mental notes about what the algorithm had told him about Maya when she walked in.

Actually, she didn't walk. She sort of... burst in, like the weather.

She was shorter than he'd expected, wearing a flowy rust-colored top over black jeans and boots that looked broken-in from actual travel, not fashion. Her hair was up in that same messy bun from her photos, held in place with what appeared to be a pencil. She had a camera strap across her chest and was already smiling—not at him yet, but at the world in general, like being alive at 10:02 AM on a Saturday was inherently amusing.

When she spotted him and her eyes met his, Derek felt his carefully prepared greeting dissolve entirely.

"Hi," she said, arriving at the table with an energy that made his coffee seem to vibrate in sympathy. "I'm Maya. You must be my 97.8% compatible nightmare."

Derek blinked. "That's... one way to start."

"Sorry." She dropped into the chair across from him, already pulling out her phone. "Is it okay if I—I'm just putting this on silent. Well, vibrate. I can't do full silent, it stresses me out, but I won't check it. Probably." She looked up. "Sorry, you were saying?"

"I wasn't—" Derek adjusted his glasses. "I hadn't said anything yet."

"Right. Okay. Hi. Fresh start." She stuck out her hand. "Maya Reyes. Professional commitment-phobe, according to my best friend. You?"

Her handshake was firm but quick, and Derek noticed she had silver rings on three fingers and chipped red nail polish. "Derek Chen. I'm... not sure how to follow that introduction."

"Try honesty. It's what the algorithm wants, right?" She was still smiling, but Derek detected something underneath it—nervousness, maybe, or the same uncertainty he was feeling.

"Okay. Derek Chen. I'm apparently boring, according to my ex-fiancée."

Maya's eyebrows shot up. "Ex-fiancée? That's buried kind of deep for a first date reveal."

"You started with commitment-phobe."

"Touché." She leaned back, studying him with an intensity that made Derek want to straighten his collar. "So. Venture capital finance guy meets professional wanderer. The algorithm thinks this works. Thoughts?"

Derek chose his words carefully. "I think... there's been a mistake."

He expected her to look offended. Instead, she laughed—loud and genuine, the kind of laugh that made several people at nearby tables turn and smile reflexively.

"Oh thank god," Maya said. "I thought I was the only one thinking that. I mean, look at us. I literally just got back from jumping off a cliff in Thailand, and you—" she gestured at him, "—you look like you've never been late for anything in your entire life."

"I haven't," Derek said, then immediately regretted it. "I mean, not that that's... good or..."

"No, own it. It's actually kind of impressive in a terrifying way." She paused. "Wait, never? Not even once?"

"Once. Third grade. My mom overslept after working a double shift. I cried in the car."

Maya's smile softened into something more genuine. "That's actually really sweet. And kind of sad."

"It was character building." Derek wasn't sure why he was telling her this. "Do you want coffee? I should have asked earlier. I just—"

"Got here early and needed to secure the optimal table position?" Maya's eyes sparkled. "I noticed. This is a good table. Very defensible. Clear sight lines to both exits."

Derek felt heat creep up his neck. "That's not—"

"I'm not making fun of you. Well, maybe a little. But in a nice way." She stood up. "I'm getting one of those ridiculously complicated drinks with like, four modifiers. Want anything?"

"I already have coffee."

"Right. Okay. Don't go anywhere." She headed toward the counter, then turned back. "That was a joke. You're clearly not going anywhere. You probably got here at 9:53."

"9:51," Derek said before he could stop himself.

Her laugh followed her to the counter.

Derek watched her order—animated hand gestures, charming the barista into what looked like a complicated conversation about oat milk versus almond milk—and tried to understand what was happening. The algorithm had said 97.8% compatible. But compatibility was supposed to be about shared values, communication styles, life goals. Maya Reyes seemed to share exactly none of his values, her communication style was chaos, and her life goal appeared to be avoiding having goals.

His phone buzzed. A message from Marcus: *How's it going? She hot?*

Derek typed back: *This was a mistake.*

Marcus: *That hot huh*

Derek put his phone face-down on the table.

Maya returned with something that looked less like coffee and more like a dessert in a cup—whipped cream, caramel drizzle, what might have been chocolate shavings. She caught him staring at it.

"Yes, I know it's basically a milkshake. No, I don't care. Life's too short for black coffee at 10 AM on a Saturday." She took a sip, got whipped cream on her nose, wiped it off unselfconsciously. "So. How do we do this?"

"Do what?"

"Prove the algorithm wrong." She pulled out her phone, started scrolling. "I'm thinking we document the whole thing. Show people that AI matchmaking is bullshit. Could be good content—'I Let a Robot Ruin My Love Life for 30 Days.'"

Derek felt something tighten in his chest. "You want to document this? Publicly?"

"I mean, yeah. That's what I do. Is that weird?" She looked up, actually uncertain for the first time. "If you're not comfortable with it—"

"No, it's..." Derek tried to organize his thoughts. Content creation. Public documentation. This was so far outside his comfort zone it might as well be on another planet. But Marcus had told him to try. Elena had called him predictable. The algorithm had given him this match for a reason, even if that reason was currently incomprehensible. "It's fine. If that's what you want."

"It's not about what I want. Well, it kind of is, but—" She shook her head. "Okay, here's my pitch. We do this properly. Ten dates, following whatever the app suggests. We document it—mostly my side, unless you want in on the content, which, no pressure. At the end of thirty days, we present our evidence that the algorithm failed spectacularly, and we both get something out of it. I get content, you get... I don't know, what do you get?"

Derek thought about it. "Proof that I tried something unpredictable?"

"There you go. Win-win." She extended her hand across the table. "Deal?"

Derek looked at her hand—those silver rings, that chipped nail polish, the easy confidence in her smile that suggested she'd never second-guessed a decision in her life. Everything about this was a bad idea. They had nothing in common. This would be a disaster.

He shook her hand anyway.

"Deal. But I have conditions."

"Oh, this should be good." Maya pulled out her phone, opened her notes app. "Hit me."

"First, nothing that could affect my job. No content that shows my workplace or identifies my company."

"Totally fair. Next?"

"Second, I need advance notice for dates. At least 24 hours. I have a schedule."

"The app won't always give us that much warning."

Derek adjusted his glasses. "Then I'll be flexible within reason."

"'Flexible within reason,'" Maya repeated, typing. "Got it. That's very on-brand for you. What else?"

"That's it for now."

"Okay. My turn. First, honesty. If this isn't working for you, you tell me. No polite suffering through dates just to be nice."

"Agreed."

"Second, you have to actually try. No showing up physically but checking out mentally. I've dated enough emotionally unavailable guys to spot it a mile away."

Something in her voice made Derek look up sharply. There was real hurt underneath the casual delivery, quickly covered but definitely there.

"I'll try," he said, meaning it. "What's your third condition?"

"That's it. Just two." She took another sip of her drink, leaving a small whipped cream mustache that she didn't notice this time. "Oh wait, actually, three. If at any point you want to bail, no judgment. Just say the word and we're done. Life's too short to waste time on people who don't want to be there."

Derek reached across the table and pointed at his own upper lip.

Maya frowned, confused, then touched her face and found the whipped cream. "Oh my god." She laughed, wiping it away with her napkin. "This is why I can't have nice things. Or adult beverages. Or apparently, first dates."

"It's fine," Derek said, and surprised himself by meaning it. "It's... humanizing."

"Humanizing. Wow. Really sweeping me off my feet here, Chen."

"Sorry, I didn't—"

"I'm joking." Her phone buzzed on the table. She glanced at it, then flipped it face-down without checking. "Sorry. Bad habit. What were we—oh, right. So what does the algorithm want us to do after this?"

Derek pulled out his own phone, opened the Synapse app. "It says we should..." He paused, reading. "Share something personal. Something we wouldn't normally tell a stranger."

"Oh good. Vulnerability exercises. My favorite." But Maya's tone was light, and she was already thinking, tapping her fingers on the table. "Okay. You first."

"Why me?"

"Because you're the one who's early to everything and probably already has an answer prepared."

She wasn't wrong. Derek had seen this prompt in the app last night and had spent twenty minutes considering what to share. But now, sitting across from this woman who somehow made chaos look effortless, his prepared answer seemed hollow.

"I color-code my calendar," he said instead. "Different colors for different types of activities. Work is blue. Personal is green. Meals are yellow. Exercise is orange. Social is purple, though that doesn't come up often."

Maya stared at him. "That's what you're going with? Calendar organization?"

"You said something personal."

"I meant like, childhood trauma or secret fears or—" She stopped, studying his face. "Oh. That is personal for you, isn't it?"

Derek felt exposed in a way he hadn't anticipated. "After my parents divorced, everything was chaos. We moved constantly. I never knew what was happening next. The color-coding... it helps me feel in control."

The table was quiet for a moment. A espresso machine hissed in the background. Someone laughed at the counter.

"Okay," Maya said softly. "That's actually really personal. Thank you for sharing that."

"Your turn."

She bit her lip, considering. "I can't stay in one place for more than six weeks. I've tried. I start feeling like the walls are closing in, like I'm missing something happening somewhere else. My therapist thinks it's because I'm afraid if I stop moving, I'll have to actually deal with..." She gestured vaguely. "Stuff."

"What kind of stuff?"

"The kind that requires a second date to unpack." But she smiled when she said it, and Derek found himself smiling back.

His phone buzzed. A notification from Synapse: Connection detected. Date #1 complete. Next sync session will be scheduled within 72 hours. Stand by.

Maya's phone buzzed simultaneously. She checked it, showed him the matching notification. "Huh. I guess we passed."

"Apparently." Derek looked at his watch—10:47 AM. They'd been talking for forty-five minutes, and his carefully scheduled grocery shopping time was now starting. But for the first time in recent memory, Derek found he didn't want to leave just to maintain his schedule.

"So," Maya said, gathering her things. "This was... not as terrible as I expected?"

"That's a ringing endorsement."

"From me? It kind of is." She stood, slinging her camera strap over her shoulder. "See you at date number two, I guess.

Try not to spend the next 72 hours color-coding your feelings about this."

"I'll do my best."

She was halfway to the door when she turned back. "Hey, Derek?"

"Yeah?"

"For what it's worth, I don't think you're boring. Structured, maybe. Possibly a little terrifying in your organization. But not boring."

She left before he could respond, the door chiming behind her.

Derek sat there for another moment, looking at his now-cold coffee, his precisely positioned chair, his phone showing the successful date notification. Marcus would want a full debrief. His calendar was now off by forty-seven minutes. He had emails to answer, meal prep to complete, a run to log.

But first, he opened his notes app and typed: *Maya Reyes. Not what I expected. Might be exactly what I needed.*

He deleted it immediately.

Then typed it again.

Left it there.

Maya

"So?" Suzie asked the moment Maya got in the car. "How bad was it?"

Maya buckled her seatbelt, trying to organize her thoughts. "It was... weird?"

"Weird bad or weird good?"

"Both? Neither? I don't know." Maya pulled out her phone, scrolled through the photos she'd taken when Derek wasn't looking—not of him directly, but of his coffee cup (black, simple, already empty), his watch (practical, classic), his posture (impeccable, like he'd never slouched in his life). "He's so... organized. Like, Suzie, he color-codes his calendar. Different colors for different activities."

"That's not that weird. I color-code my—"

"He apologized for not asking if I wanted coffee before he ordered his own. Who does that?"

"Polite people?"

"He was early. Like, really early. I bet he got there at—" Maya checked the timestamp on one of her photos, "—9:51. Who arrives nine minutes early to a first date?"

Suzie pulled out of the parking spot. "Someone who takes things seriously?"

"That's what's weird!" Maya twisted in her seat to face her friend. "He takes everything seriously. Every answer was so thoughtful and measured. And then I'd say something and he'd look at me like I was speaking a different language, but not in a bad way. More like... confused but curious?"

"You like him."

"What? No. I just said we have nothing in common."

"You've been talking nonstop for five minutes about someone you supposedly have nothing in common with."

Maya opened her mouth to argue, then closed it. She pulled up Derek's profile again, studied his photos. In every single one, he looked composed. Put together. Like someone who'd never made an impulsive decision, never missed a flight, never had to buy a replacement phone charger in an airport at 3 AM because he'd left his somewhere in Prague.

"He's the opposite of every guy I've ever dated," Maya said finally.

"I know."

"Like, the complete opposite. He probably has a retirement account. And health insurance that isn't just 'hoping nothing bad happens.'"

"Probably."

"His last relationship was a three-year engagement that ended a year ago. He's looking for something serious. I can barely commit to dinner plans."

"Uh-huh."

Maya looked at her friend. "You're doing that thing where you let me talk myself into something."

"Am I?" Suzie's expression was perfectly innocent.

"We have nine more dates. The algorithm is clearly broken. We're going to prove it, and then this will all be over."

"If you say so."

"I do say so." Maya opened Instagram, started drafting a post about the date. She selected the photo of Derek's coffee cup—artistic, not invasive—and started typing:

> *Date #1 with my "97.8% compatible" match. He drinks black coffee and arrives early. I drink caffeinated desserts and barely arrive at all. The algorithm thinks this works. We're going to prove it wrong. Stay tuned for the disaster. #SynapseExperiment, #AIDating*
>
> *#ThisShouldBeInteresting*

Her finger hovered over "post."

She thought about Derek's face when he'd talked about his color-coded calendar, the vulnerability in admitting why he needed that control. The way he'd pointed at his own lip to tell her about the whipped cream instead of just letting her be embarrassed. The fact that he'd agreed to try something completely outside his comfort zone just because his brother thought he should.

He's not boring, she'd told him.

She believed it.

Maya edited the caption:

> *Date #1 with my "97.8% compatible" match. He's structured. I'm chaos. The algorithm has theories. So do I. Let's see who's right.*
>
> *#SynapseExperiment*

She posted it before she could overthink it.

Her phone immediately started buzzing with notifications. Comments, likes, DMs from people wanting updates. This was what she did—shared her life, turned experiences into content, kept moving forward.

So why did she feel like she'd just started something she couldn't control?

Derek

Derek made it home by 11:15, which threw off his meal prep schedule by exactly one hour and fifteen minutes. He could adjust. Extend his afternoon "flex time" into the meal prep window, shift everything back. It would work.

He was reorganizing his calendar when Marcus FaceTimed.

"Well?" His brother's face filled the screen, eager and nosy. "How'd it go?"

"It was fine."

"'Fine.' Bro, you agreed to a multidate social experiment with a woman you have nothing in common with, and you're going with 'fine'?"

Derek set his phone on the counter, started pulling out meal prep containers. "What do you want me to say?"

"I want you to say she was amazing or terrible or literally anything with some emotion attached."

"She was..." Derek paused, trying to find the right words while measuring rice. "Unexpected."

"Unexpected good?"

"Just unexpected." Derek focused on his measurements. "She wants to document the whole thing. Turn it into content for her followers."

"Oh shit, really? That's actually kind of cool. You gonna be internet famous?"

"No. I'm staying mostly off-camera. But she's going to post about the dates, prove the algorithm wrong."

Marcus was quiet for a moment. "You think the algorithm's wrong?"

Derek thought about Maya's laugh, the whipped cream mustache, the way she'd understood without judgment why calendar organization was personal for him. "I don't know. We're very different."

"Different how?"

"Every way. She's spontaneous, I'm structured. She travels constantly, I like routine. She makes decisions on impulse, I analyze everything. She—"

"Sounds like she balances you out."

"Or we're incompatible."

"Maybe that's the same thing." Marcus shifted, and Derek could see he was in his studio apartment in Oakland, equipment and cables visible in the background. "Look, man, Elena was perfect on paper, right? Same industry, same values, same life goals. You guys were so compatible it was boring. And it still didn't work."

"That's not—"

"Maybe the algorithm knows that 'compatible' doesn't mean 'identical.' Maybe it means finding someone who challenges you to be better." Marcus's voice softened. "Just... try to actually be present for this, okay? Don't just show up physically while your brain runs calculations about why it won't work."

After they hung up, Derek stood in his kitchen surrounded by perfectly portioned meals and thought about Maya's third condition: If at any point you want to bail, no judgment. Just say the word and we're done. Life's too short to waste time on people who don't want to be there.

He'd heard the story underneath that condition—years of people who'd left, who hadn't chosen to stay, who'd proven that movement was safer than staying still.

Derek pulled out his phone, navigated to Instagram, and after a moment's hesitation, found Maya's profile. Her latest post showed his coffee cup, her caption talking about structure versus chaos. The comments were already flooding in:

> *@SuzieParksPhotography: Called it*
> *@wanderlust_adventures: This is gonna be good*
> *@techbro_takes: As someone who also color-codes calendars, I feel attacked*
> *@maya_superfan_01: PLEASE tell me there's gonna be a date #2*

Derek clicked "follow" before he could overthink it.

His phone buzzed immediately. A DM from Maya: *Did you just follow me? That was fast. Algorithm must've pinged you :).*

Derek typed back: *Just doing research. If we're documenting this, I should know what I'm getting into.*

Maya: Smart. *Very on-brand. FYI, I don't post anything you're uncomfortable with. I know I joked about it, but seriously, your privacy matters.*

Derek stared at that message for a long moment. She barely knew him, but she'd already identified what would matter to him and addressed it directly.

He typed: *I trust you.* Then, before he could delete it: See *you at date #2.*

Maya: *Try not to plan it to death before the app even tells us what it is*

Derek: *No promises*

Maya: *At least you're honest*

Derek put his phone down and returned to his meal prep, but his mind was elsewhere.

Ten dates. Thirty days. A woman who made chaos look effortless and who somehow, impossibly, had gotten him to share something real within the first hour of meeting. This was either going to be the best decision he'd made in years or the worst.

Marcus would say that uncertainty meant he was actually living.

Elena would say he was being reckless.

The algorithm was betting on something Derek couldn't quite articulate yet. He portioned out his meals: Monday through Thursday, lunch and dinner, everything labeled and dated.

The thing was, Derek had always believed in systems. Systems kept the world predictable, manageable, safe. His color-coded calendar, his meal prep routine, his morning coffee at exactly 6:47 AM—these weren't compulsions, they were scaffolding. They held him upright when everything else threatened to tilt.

But Maya had walked into his carefully constructed universe and smiled at it like it was charming instead of concerning, asked him questions that bypassed his defenses entirely, and somehow made him want to step outside the scaffolding to see what else was out there.

It was terrifying. It was also, if he was being honest with himself in the quiet of his kitchen with the Tupperware lids clicking into place, a little bit thrilling.

But when he opened his calendar to adjust his schedule, he left Saturday afternoon blank. Just in case.

***

3. When It Works (Until It Doesn't)

Three Weeks Later

DATES #4-7

Date #4: Hiking at Rancho San Antonio

Saturday Morning, Two Weeks After The Escape Room

Derek had suggested they meet at the trailhead at 7:00 AM. Maya had countered with 8:30. They'd compromised on 7:45, and Maya had actually shown up at 7:52—a personal record, she'd claimed.

"You're wearing hiking boots," Derek observed as she approached, two coffee cups in hand.

"Don't sound so shocked. I do occasionally wear appropriate footwear." She handed him one of the cups—black coffee, no sugar, exactly how he took it. She'd remembered. "I've hiked all over Southeast Asia. I can handle a California trail."

"I didn't say you couldn't."

"You were thinking it."

"I was thinking you look nice." Derek adjusted his backpack straps, feeling his ears heat. "The boots are practical. That's all."

Maya's expression softened into something genuine. "You're sweet when you're awkward. Has anyone told you that?"

"No one's called me sweet before."

"Well, you are. Come on, nature boy. Show me this trail you've been talking about."

The hike had been Derek's suggestion—something active, outdoors, with clear goals and measurable progress. What he hadn't anticipated was how much he'd enjoy watching Maya experience it.

She photographed everything: the light filtering through oak trees, a deer they spotted in the distance, the view from Deer Hollow Farm overlook. But unlike her usual content creation mode, she wasn't performing. She'd just point at things and say, "Look at that," with genuine wonder, like she was discovering the trail existed for the first time.

"You've really never been here?" Derek asked when they stopped for water at the two-mile marker.

"I've been to twenty-three countries but I've barely explored my own backyard. It's embarrassing, actually." Maya sat on a boulder, tilting her face toward the sun. "I'm always looking for the next big adventure somewhere else. I forget there's stuff right here."

Derek sat beside her, close enough that their shoulders almost touched. "Why do you do that? Always look somewhere else?"

"Therapy question?"

"Curious question."

Maya was quiet for a moment, watching a group of cyclists pass on the adjacent path. "When I was in college, my lola—my grandmother—got sick. Cancer. I was supposed to study abroad in Spain that semester, but I stayed home to help take care of her. Watched her get weaker every day, felt the walls closing in. I promised myself that after she died, I'd never let myself get stuck like that again."

"Maya, that's not—"

"I know. I know it's not rational. But ever since then, staying in one place too long makes me feel like I'm waiting for something bad to happen." She looked at him. "Your turn. Why do you need everything so organized?"

Derek had known this was coming—they'd been trading vulnerabilities like currency for three weeks now. "After my parents split, my mom couldn't afford our house in Palo Alto. We moved eight times in seven years. Different schools, different neighborhoods, different routines every time. I never knew what was coming next, never felt settled. The organization—the color-coded calendar, the meal prep, all of it—it's my way of knowing what happens next."

"Control."

"Predictability," Derek corrected. "There's a difference."

"Is there?"

"Predictability is about reducing anxiety. Control is about power." He paused. "Though I guess they're related."

Maya bumped his shoulder with hers. "We're both kind of messed up, huh?"

"Complementarily messed up," Derek said. "According to the algorithm."

"The algorithm might be onto something." She stood, offering him her hand. "Come on. Let's see if you can keep up with this international hiker."

She'd made it another mile before admitting the trail was harder than she'd expected. Derek had offered to carry her backpack, and she'd refused on principle, but accepted his hand on the steeper sections. By the time they'd reached the summit—a modest peak with views of the South Bay—they were both slightly breathless and grinning.

"Okay," Maya admitted, taking photos of the vista. "This was worth the early wake-up."

"I told you."

"Don't gloat. It's not attractive." But she was smiling as she took a selfie of them both, the valley spread out behind them. "Date number four: successful. The algorithm remains undefeated."

Synapse notification: Date #4 complete. Compatibility: 98.6%. Shared experience multiplier activated.

Date #5: Farmers Market + Cooking Together

Sunday Morning, One Week Later

This date hadn't been scheduled by Synapse. Derek had texted Maya on Wednesday night:

Derek: *What are you doing Sunday morning?*

Maya: *Probably sleeping until noon. Why?*

Derek: *Want to go to the farmers market? We could get ingredients and cook something together. My place.*

Maya: *Derek Chen, are you asking me on a NON-ALGORITHM date?*

Derek: *I'm supplementing the algorithm's schedule with additional compatible activities*

Maya: *That's the most romantically structured sentence I've ever received*

Derek: *Is that a yes?*

Maya: *It's a definitely yes*

The Mountain View Farmers Market was crowded with the Sunday morning crowd—young families, elderly couples, tech workers in athleisure picking up prepared foods. Maya moved through the stalls with the same enthusiasm she brought to everything, stopping to sample cheese, examine heirloom tomatoes, debate the merits of various mushroom varieties.

"You're very decisive here," Derek observed as she confidently selected vegetables.

"Food is important. I don't mess around." She held up two bunches of basil. "Which one?"

"They look identical."

"This one has darker leaves. Better flavor." She bought three bunches. "We're making pesto. Fresh pasta if you have a roller, regular pasta if you don't."

"I have a roller."

"Of course you do." But she was grinning. "What else should we get? Burrata? Prosciutto? Oh, look—fresh bread!"

They ended up with two bags full of ingredients, having spent an hour wandering through the market. Derek realized halfway through that he'd forgotten to check his watch even once, had missed his usual Saturday run time entirely, and didn't care.

At his apartment—which Maya immediately dubbed "aggressively organized"—they cooked together with the easy rhythm they'd developed at the cooking class. Maya made the pesto from scratch, filling his kitchen with the scent of basil and garlic. Derek rolled out pasta dough with precise, even pressure while she told him about a disastrous cooking attempt in a hostel kitchen in Portugal.

"So there I am, at 2 AM, trying to explain to the hostel manager that the smoke alarm went off because I was making adobo, not because the building was on fire—"

"How do you set off a smoke alarm making adobo?"

"Enthusiastic searing!" Maya was crushing garlic with the side of a knife, somehow making even that look chaotic but effective. "The point is, I'm banned from three hostels in Lisbon now."

"Three?"

"It's a long story involving separate incidents."

Derek laughed—the full, genuine laugh that still surprised him when it happened. Maya looked up, caught his expression.

"What?"

"Nothing. I just—" He shook his head. "I don't laugh this much normally."

"Yeah?" She set down the knife, moved closer. They were in his small kitchen, the counter covered in ingredients, flour dusting the air between them. "Maybe you should normally."

"Maybe I should."

They were standing very close now. Derek could count the flour specks in Maya's hair, could see the exact shade of her eyes in the afternoon light coming through his kitchen window. Her hand was still holding the knife, but she set it down carefully on the cutting board without looking away from him.

"Derek—" she started.

His phone timer went off—the pasta water was boiling.

They both laughed, the moment breaking but not disappearing, just transforming into something else. They finished cooking, ate at his small dining table while she told him more ridiculous travel stories and he admitted to some of his more embarrassing workplace moments. When she left that evening, she kissed his cheek at the door—quick, casual, but it sent electricity through his entire nervous system.

After she left, Derek found himself staring at his meticulously organized kitchen, now slightly chaotic with their cooking debris, and thinking it had never looked better.

No Synapse notification. This one was just theirs.

Date #6: Comedy Show in San Francisco

Friday Night, Mid-Week

The Synapse notification had come on Tuesday:

SYNC SESSION #6 SCHEDULED
Activity: Live Comedy Performance
Location: Punch Line Comedy Club - San Francisco
Friday, 8:00 PM
Note: Laughter is a compatibility indicator. Shared humor deepens bonds.

"*The algorithm wants to see if we have the same sense of humor,*" Maya had texted him immediately.

Derek: *What if we don't?*

Maya: *Then we've been faking laughter for five dates and we're both great actors*

Derek: *Have you been faking?*

Maya: *Not even a little bit*

The comedy club was packed, filled with the Friday night energy of people ready to laugh after a long work week. They'd arrived early enough to get decent seats—Derek's planning, Maya's willingness to actually be on time for once.

The opening act was good. The second act was better. But the headliner—a woman in her forties doing a bit about dating app disasters—had them both crying with laughter.

"And he shows up with a BINDER," the comedian was saying. "A three-ring binder labeled 'Getting to Know You: Structured Edition.' I'm not joking. He had tabs. COLOR-CODED TABS."

Derek felt Maya glance at him, and he looked back, both of them grinning. She reached over and took his hand, lacing their fingers together, and Derek felt something settle in his chest—like a puzzle piece clicking into place.

The comedian continued: "I'm like, sir, this is a coffee date, not a business meeting. And he says—I will never forget this—he says, 'I prefer to optimize the getting-to-know-you process.' OPTIMIZE. Like I'm a quarterly earnings report!"

The whole club was laughing, but Derek barely heard the rest. Maya was leaning into him, her shoulder against his, her hand warm in his, and he thought: *This is what happiness feels like.*

After the show, they walked through San Francisco's North Beach neighborhood, neither quite ready for the night to end.

"That guy sounded familiar," Maya teased, squeezing his hand.

"I have never brought a binder to a date."

"But you've thought about it."

"...I've considered making an agenda."

Maya stopped walking, staring at him. "Derek Chen. Tell me you did not almost bring an agenda to our first date."

"I didn't! I just... thought about what topics we should cover. In my head. Which I then organized into categories. Mentally."

"You're ridiculous."

"You knew this about me."

"I did. And somehow—" She stepped closer, looking up at him. They were on a relatively quiet street corner, the city humming around them but feeling distant. "—I like you anyway."

"Anyway? Or because of it?"

"Definitely because of it." She rose on her toes slightly. "Is this okay?"

Derek answered by closing the distance between them.

Their first real kiss happened on a San Francisco street corner with the smell of garlic from a nearby Italian restaurant and the sound of distant traffic. It was soft and tentative and perfect, and when they pulled apart, Maya was smiling.

"The algorithm definitely planned that," she said.

"The algorithm has good timing."

"Come on, let's get you back to Mountain View before you turn into a pumpkin."

They held hands on the entire drive back, and when Derek got home, he found himself touching his lips like a teenager, unable to stop smiling.

Synapse notification: Date #6 complete. Compatibility: 98.8%. Physical connection established. Emotional integration proceeding optimally.

Date #7: Bookstore + Coffee

Lazy Sunday Afternoon

This wasn't a Synapse date either. Maya had texted him Saturday night:

Maya: *Tomorrow. Kepler's Books. Noon. Bring your overthinking brain and your credit card.*

Derek: *Why my credit card?*

Maya: *Because I'm going to show you my favorite section and you're going to show me yours and we're each buying the other a book. It's a thing.*

Derek: *What thing?*

Maya: *A relationship thing. Keep up, Derek.*

Kepler's Books in Menlo Park was packed with Sunday browsers. Maya led him straight to the travel section, pulling books with practiced ease.

"This one—" She handed him a book about train journeys through Asia. "—changed how I think about slow travel. And this one—" A memoir about walking across Spain. "—made me cry in a good way."

Derek examined both books, reading jacket copy carefully. "You want me to buy you travel books when you've already traveled everywhere?"

"I want you to understand why I love it. And—" She grabbed another book, something about the philosophy of wandering. "—maybe you'll get the urge to go somewhere unplanned."

"That seems unlikely."

"A girl can dream." She gestured toward the rest of the store. "Your turn. Show me your section."

Derek led her to the business and economics area, but then veered left into fiction.

"Plot twist," Maya said. "The finance guy reads novels."

"I contain multitudes," Derek said, echoing her words from weeks ago. He scanned the shelves, pulled out a worn paperback. "This one. It's about an architect who designs buildings but can't design his own life. It's about structure and chaos and finding meaning in both."

Maya took the book carefully, reading the first page while standing there in the aisle. "Derek, this is beautiful."

"I thought you'd like it."

"I do. I really do." She looked up at him. "Can I tell you something?"

"Always."

"I'm usually the person recommending books to people. No one really recommends books to me. They assume I only care about travel guides and airport thrillers."

"You're more than your Instagram feed."

"I know. But most people don't."

Derek pulled her into a hug right there in the middle of the fiction section, not caring who saw. "I'm not most people."

"No," Maya said against his chest. "You're really not."

They bought each other's books, then got coffee at the in-store café. Maya read the first chapter of her new book while Derek worked through the introduction of his. Occasionally, one of them would read a passage aloud. It was quiet and comfortable and domestic in a way that should have terrified Derek but somehow didn't.

"This is nice," Maya said eventually, closing her book.

"Yeah?"

"Yeah. Just... existing together. Not doing anything Instagram-worthy. Just reading."

"You could post about it."

"I don't want to." She reached across the table, took his hand. "Some things can just be ours."

Derek felt something shift in his chest—a recalibration of what he wanted, what he was building with her. "I like that."

"Me too."

No notification needed. They knew this one was working.

Present Day: Three Weeks After The Escape Room

Maya

Maya was editing photos from the farmers market date—sun-drenched shots of vegetables, a candid of Derek examining tomatoes with scientific precision—when her phone rang. Not a text. An actual phone call.

From *Elena Volkov.*

Maya stared at the name on her screen. She'd never spoken to Derek's ex, had only seen her in carefully composed Instagram photos and that one comment on Derek's post. They weren't connected on social media. They had no reason to communicate.

She almost didn't answer.

"Hello?"

"Maya? Hi, this is Elena Volkov." The voice was warm, professional, with the slight formality of someone who practiced perfect diction. "I hope I'm not interrupting."

"I was just working. It's fine." Maya closed her laptop, suddenly on alert. "How did you get my number?"

"James Park—Derek's friend. We've been... well, that's actually why I'm calling." A pause. "Can we meet for coffee? I promise this isn't weird. Or maybe it is weird, but it's important."

Derek

Derek was in a Monday morning meeting when the Synapse notification came through. He normally kept his phone on silent during work hours, but he'd started making an exception for messages from Maya and Synapse alerts. His colleagues had noticed but hadn't commented.

He glanced at it discreetly:

> *SYNC SESSION #8 SCHEDULED*
> *Activity: Double Date Experience*
> *Location: The Plumed Horse - Saratoga*
> *Friday, 7:30 PM*
> *Additional participants: James Park & Elena Volkov*
> *Note: Testing relationship resilience in complex social dynamics. Your match strength will be evaluated in the presence of previous relational history.*

Derek's stomach dropped. Elena. James. A double date!

His phone buzzed immediately with texts:

James: *Dude. DUDE. I need to talk to you.*

Maya: *Did you see?? ELENA? Your ex Elena??*

Marcus: *The algorithm is MESSY. I respect it.*

Derek excused himself from the meeting, stepping into an empty conference room. He called James first.

"What the hell is going on?" Derek demanded.

"I know, I know—listen, I was going to tell you." James sounded stressed. "Synapse matched me with Elena three weeks ago. We've been on a few dates. It's been... good? Really good, actually. But I didn't know how to tell you, and then the app scheduled this double date thing and—"

"You're dating my ex-fiancée."

"I'm dating someone the algorithm matched me with who happens to be your ex-fiancée." James paused. "Derek, if this is too weird, I'll cancel. I'll tell her we can't do this. You're my best friend. You come first."

Derek leaned against the conference room table, trying to process. Elena was with James. The algorithm had matched them. And now Synapse wanted all four of them—Derek, Maya, James, Elena—to have dinner together to "test relationship resilience."

"Does Maya know?"

"I don't know. Probably? The notification went to everyone."

Derek hung up and immediately called Maya. She answered on the first ring.

"So," she said without preamble, "your ex-fiancée wants to have dinner with us."

"James is my best friend."

"Your best friend is dating your ex-fiancée."

"Apparently."

A long pause. Derek could hear traffic in the background—Maya was driving, probably heading to meet Suzie or run an errand.

"Are you okay?" Maya asked, her voice softer. "This is a lot."

"I don't know," Derek admitted. "Elena and I ended a year ago. I'm over her. I've moved on. But seeing her with James, having dinner together—"

"—is the algorithm's way of testing whether you're really over her. And whether I'm secure enough to handle it." Maya's voice had an edge to it. "Classic relationship stress test."

"We don't have to go."

"Don't we though?" She was quiet for a moment. "Derek, we've had seven dates, and they've all been perfect. We've been in this bubble where everything works. Maybe the algorithm knows it's time to see if this holds up when things get complicated."

"Or we could stay in the bubble."

"That's not real life." Maya sighed. "Look, Elena called me this morning."

"What?"

"Yeah. She wants to meet for coffee before Friday. She said it's important." Another pause. "Should I go?"

Derek thought about it. His instinct was to say no, to keep Maya and Elena in separate compartments of his life. But Maya was right—they couldn't stay in the bubble forever.

"If you want to go, go," he said. "I trust you."

"Yeah?"

"Yeah." And he meant it.

After they hung up, Derek sat in the empty conference room, staring at the Synapse notification. The algorithm had been right about everything so far—the compatibility, the dates, the way he and Maya complemented each other. But this felt different. This felt like manipulation.

His phone buzzed. A text from Elena: *I know this is strange. I want to explain before Friday. Can we talk?*

Derek stared at the message for a long moment before typing back: *Thursday lunch. My office building café. 12:30.*

He returned to his meeting, but his mind was elsewhere, running scenarios and calculations the way he always did when he felt control slipping away.

The bubble was bursting. The real test was beginning.

Maya

Maya met Elena on Tuesday afternoon at a small café in Los Altos—neutral territory, halfway between Mountain View and wherever Elena worked (Google's main campus, according to her Instagram).

Elena arrived exactly on time, of course. She was even more striking in person—tall, elegant, wearing a cream-colored sweater and minimal jewelry. She looked like someone who had their life together in a way Maya never quite managed.

"Thank you for meeting me," Elena said, sitting down with a perfectly composed latte. "I know this must be strange."

"That's one word for it." Maya wrapped her hands around her own drink—iced coffee, messy and cold even though it was a chilly day. "Why did you want to talk?"

"Because I owe you context." Elena took a careful sip. "James and I were matched by Synapse three weeks ago. I didn't know he was Derek's best friend at first—we have different last names, and it didn't come up until our second date. By then, we'd already... connected."

"And you didn't think to tell Derek?"

"James wanted to. I asked him to wait." Elena met Maya's eyes directly. "I needed to figure out if this was real or if I was just comfortable with James because he reminded me of Derek. I needed to be sure before we complicated things."

"And are you sure?"

"Yes." No hesitation. "James is not Derek. He's different in ways that work better for me. But I also know that seeing us together is going to be hard for Derek, and by extension, hard for you."

Maya studied Elena, trying to understand her angle. "Why are you telling me this?"

"Because I care about Derek. Not romantically—I'm genuinely over that—but he was part of my life for three years. I want him to be happy." Elena paused. "And you make him happy. I can see it in his Instagram posts, in the way he talks about you when James mentions you. But this double date is going to test that, and I wanted you to know that James and I are real. We're not some algorithm glitch or rebound relationship."

"The algorithm matched you both," Maya said slowly. "Just like it matched Derek and me."

"Yes. And if the algorithm is right about you two, it's right about us." Elena's expression was serious. "But Maya, I also need to ask you something, and I need you to be honest."

"Okay."

"Are you in this with Derek? Really in this? Or are you going to run when things get hard?" Elena's voice was gentle but firm. "Because Derek doesn't deserve someone else leaving him. And if you're going to leave, do it now, before Friday, before he's in deeper."

Maya felt anger flash through her. "You don't know me."

"No, I don't. But I know Derek. And I know what it did to him when I left. He'll survive if this doesn't work out, but I'd rather he not have to."

Elena stood, gathering her things. "Think about it. If you're not ready to stay—if you're going to pick adventure over him when it comes down to it—that's okay. But let him go now."

She left cash on the table and walked out, leaving Maya sitting alone with her melting iced coffee and a lot of uncomfortable questions.

Derek

Derek met Elena on Thursday, as planned, at the café in his office building. She looked the same—composed, elegant, slightly distant in the way she'd always been. But there was something different too. Something lighter.

"You look well," Elena said as they sat down.

"So do you." Derek had his usual black coffee, was trying not to seem as nervous as he felt. "James told me about the match."

"I wanted to tell you myself, but..." Elena shook her head. "Derek, I'm sorry. This must be incredibly awkward."

"It's definitely not not awkward." He took a sip of coffee. "But James is my best friend. If the algorithm matched you two, and you're both happy, then... I'm happy for you."

"Are you though?"

Derek considered lying, decided against it. "I'm working on it. It's complicated. You and I ended badly, and seeing you with someone I care about—someone who was there during our breakup—it's a lot."

"I know. That's why I wanted to talk before Friday." Elena leaned forward. "Derek, I need you to understand something. What James and I have—it's different from what you and I had. Better, actually. Not because you weren't enough, but because we weren't right for each other."

"I know that."

"Do you? Because when we broke up, you took it as confirmation that you were boring. Predictable. Not enough." Her voice was gentle. "But Derek, you weren't the problem. We were the problem. We looked perfect on paper, but we never challenged each other. We never pushed each other to grow."

"And James does that for you?"

"Yes. And from what I can see, Maya does that for you." Elena smiled slightly. "You're different now. I can see it. You're posting on Instagram. You're laughing in photos. You look... lighter."

Derek thought about the past few weeks—the hiking, the cooking, the comedy show, the kiss on a San Francisco street corner. The way Maya made him want to leave white space in his calendar, to try things without a plan, to laugh at his own rigidity.

"She does make me lighter," he admitted.

"Then hold onto that. Even when Friday is awkward. Even when seeing James and me together is weird. Because Derek, what you have with Maya—it's real. And it's worth fighting for."

After Elena left, Derek sat in the café for another twenty minutes, processing. His ex-fiancée was giving him relationship advice about his current relationship. The algorithm had orchestrated this entire situation. And somehow, despite the complexity and awkwardness, he felt... okay.

More than okay. He felt ready.

His phone buzzed. Maya: *How did it go?*

Derek: *Better than expected. You?*

Maya: *Complicated. Can I come over tonight?*

Derek: *Always*

Maya

Maya showed up at Derek's apartment at 7:30 with Thai takeout and a lot on her mind. He opened the door in sweatpants and a worn Stanford t-shirt, looking more relaxed than she'd ever seen him.

"Hey," he said, taking the food bags from her.

"Hey." She followed him inside, kicked off her shoes, made herself at home in his space the way she'd started doing over the past few weeks. "We need to talk about Friday."

"I know." Derek set out plates, distributed food with his usual precision. "Elena wanted to make sure I was okay with her and James. Which was thoughtful but also weird."

"She wanted to make sure I wasn't going to run." Maya speared a piece of chicken with more force than necessary. "She basically told me to leave you now if I'm not serious."

Derek looked up sharply. "She said that?"

"Not in those words, but yeah. She said you don't deserve someone else leaving you, and if I'm going to pick adventure over you when it comes down to it, I should let you go now."

"Maya—"

"And the thing is—" Maya set down her fork, met his eyes. "—she's not wrong. I do run. That's my thing. When things get real, when roots start forming, I panic and find a reason to leave. I've done it with jobs, with apartments, with relationships. It's my pattern."

"But you're still here."

"I'm still here," she echoed. "But Derek, what if Friday is too much? What if seeing you with Elena, even though you're over her, makes me realize that you're always going to have this history I'm not part of? What if I get scared and—"

Derek moved around the table, kneeling beside her chair so they were at eye level. "Then we'll deal with it. Together. Maya, I'm not going into Friday expecting it to be easy. It's going to be awkward and probably uncomfortable. But I'm not going with Elena. I'm going with you."

"What if the algorithm is testing whether we're really compatible?" Maya's voice was small. "What if seeing you with your perfect-on-paper ex makes me realize I'm not enough?"

"You are enough. More than enough." Derek took her hands. "Maya, Elena was perfect on paper. We had the same jobs, the same goals, the same five-year plans. And we were miserable together. You and I look wrong on paper, but we're right in every way that actually matters."

"The algorithm matched you with me. And it matched her with James."

"Exactly. The algorithm saw what we couldn't—that compatible doesn't mean identical. It means complementary." He squeezed her hands. "We can skip Friday if you want. Tell the algorithm to reschedule or cancel entirely. I care more about you being comfortable than completing some arbitrary date assignment."

Maya thought about it—really thought about it. She could run right now. Could say Friday was too much, could put distance between herself and this relationship that was getting more real every day. Could protect herself the way she always had.

Or she could stay. Could trust that what they'd built over seven dates and countless texts and spontaneous non-algorithm meetings was strong enough to handle one awkward dinner.

"No," she said finally. "We should go. We should do the hard thing."

"You're sure?"

"I'm terrified. But yeah, I'm sure." She pulled him up from his kneeling position, into her lap, wrapping her arms around him. "Besides, I want to see what the algorithm thinks is going to break us. Spite is a powerful motivator."

Derek laughed against her shoulder. "That's very on-brand for you."

"I know who I am." She pulled back to look at him. "Derek, I can't promise I won't get scared. I can't promise I won't have moments where I want to run. But I can promise I'll tell you when I'm scared instead of just disappearing."

"That's all I need."

They ate their Thai food, transitioned to the couch, ended up tangled together watching a documentary about urban planning that Derek had been excited about and Maya pretended to care about but actually found fascinating because of how much he cared about it.

"You're not watching," Derek said eventually, noticing her attention was on him rather than the screen.

"I'm watching you watch it. That's more interesting."

"Why?"

"Because you light up when you talk about things you care about. Your whole face changes. It's..." She searched for the word. "It's beautiful."

Derek went still, then turned to face her fully. "Maya Reyes, are you going soft on me?"

"Maybe. Don't tell anyone. I have a reputation to maintain."

"Your secret's safe with me." He kissed her, slow and sweet, and Maya thought: *This is what staying feels like.*

She didn't hate it.

Synapse notification that night, delivered to all four participants:

> *SYNC SESSION #8 CONFIRMED*
> *Friday, 7:30 PM, The Plumed Horse*
> *Participants: Derek Chen & Maya Reyes (Match #2847), James Park & Elena Volkov (Match #2903)*
> *Objective: Evaluate relationship resilience under*

> *complex social dynamics*
> *Note: This session is mandatory for continued algorithm participation. Non-attendance will result in match suspension.*
>
> *Additional note: Trust the process. The algorithm has brought you this far. See where it takes you next.*

Maya screenshot the notification and sent it to Suzie: *The algorithm is really leaning into the drama*

Suzie: *Or it knows exactly what you need to face*

Maya: *Why does everyone keep saying that?*

Suzie: *Because we're all watching you fall in love and trying not to jinx it*

Maya stared at that message for a long time.

Fall in love.

Was that what was happening?

She looked at Derek, now actually absorbed in his documentary, one arm draped over her shoulders like it belonged there.

Yeah. That was exactly what was happening.

And it was terrifying.

***

4. Heat and Harmony

Maya

The notification came on Tuesday morning while Maya was editing footage from a sponsored post about sustainable travel gear. Her phone buzzed, and the Synapse app icon appeared with a bright red notification badge.

SYNC SESSION #2 SCHEDULED
Activity: Culinary Creation Workshop
Location: The Kitchen Collaborative - Castro Street
Thursday, 6:30 PM
Dress code: Casual (prepare to get messy)
Note: This session focuses on complementary collaboration

Maya screenshot the notification and sent it to Derek: *Cooking class. Thursday. You're probably already adjusting your calendar*

His response came four minutes later: *Already done. I moved my evening run to morning. Do you know what we're cooking?*

Maya: *Does it matter?*

Derek: *I like to prepare*

Maya: *It's COOKING. You just... cook*

Derek: *There are techniques. Methods. Mise en place*

Maya: *Gesundheit*

Derek: *That's not... never mind. I'll see you Thursday*

Maya: *Bring your color-coded apron*

She didn't get a response to that one.

Thursday evening, Maya arrived at The Kitchen Collaborative at 6:33 PM—only three minutes late, which for her was practically early. The space was industrial-chic: exposed brick, stainless steel counters, pots and pans hanging from ceiling racks like metallic stalactites. About six other couples were already there, looking various degrees of comfortable with the setting.

Derek was at station four, of course he was, wearing dark jeans and a navy henley with the sleeves already rolled to his elbows. He'd beaten her there by—Maya checked her phone—fifteen minutes.

"You're early," she said, dropping her bag on their shared counter space.

"You're late," he replied, but his tone was mild, almost teasing.

"Three minutes is not late. Three minutes is 'fashionable timing.'" Maya grabbed one of the aprons hanging behind their station—red with white polka dots. She held up the other one, plain black. "Want to match or coordinate?"

"I'll take the black one."

"Shocking choice." But Maya was grinning as she tied on her apron. "So, what are we making? Did you sneak a peek at the menu?"

"No." Derek adjusted his apron with precise movements. "But I'm hoping for something with clear instructions."

"And I'm hoping for something we can improvise."

"Of course you are."

A woman in her forties approached the front of the room, clapping her hands once. She had short silver hair and the confidence of someone who'd spent decades in professional kitchens. "Good evening, everyone! I'm Chef Maria, and welcome to our Couples' Collaboration Workshop. Tonight, you'll be making handmade pasta with three-sauce components. The catch? Each of you only gets half the recipe."

Maya and Derek looked at each other.

"Oh no," Derek said quietly.

"Oh yes," Maya whispered back, delighted.

Chef Maria continued: "One partner makes the pasta dough and one sauce. The other makes two complementary sauces. You'll need to communicate, coordinate, and—most importantly—trust each other. Pasta-making is both science and art, and your success depends on working as a team."

She began distributing recipe cards, handing one to each person at every station. Maya got hers first: *Pasta Dough + Sage Brown Butter Sauce. Derek received his: Roasted Cherry Tomato Sauce + Lemon Cream Sauce.*

"I got the pasta," Maya said, scanning her card. "Flour, eggs, salt, olive oil. Seems straightforward."

Derek was reading his card with intensity. "I have two sauces with different timing requirements. The tomatoes need to roast for twenty minutes, but the cream sauce is last-minute."

"So we coordinate."

"Right. Coordinate." Derek looked around at the other couples, who were already diving into their recipes with various levels of chaos. "You start the pasta, I'll start the tomatoes?"

"Look at us, teamworking." Maya grabbed a large wooden board from under their counter. "Okay, so I need flour. Where's the—oh, there it is."

The next forty-five minutes were controlled chaos.

Maya approached pasta-making the way she approached most things: with enthusiasm and minimal planning. She dumped flour on the board in what she hoped was the right amount, made a well in the center, cracked eggs into it, and started mixing with her hands.

"Is that enough flour?" Derek asked from beside her, where he was carefully washing cherry tomatoes.

"Probably?"

"The recipe says 400 grams."

"I don't see a scale."

"There's one right—" Derek reached past her, pulling a digital scale from behind the olive oil. His arm brushed hers, and Maya caught a scent of something clean and cedar-like. "Here."

"Too late now. I'm committed." Maya kneaded the dough, which was definitely too sticky. "This is fine. This is totally fine."

"It's sticking to the board."

"Thank you, observation deck. Very helpful." But Maya was laughing, adding pinches of flour, trying to get the consistency right through feel rather than measurement.

Derek had moved to the stove, heating a pan for his tomatoes. He worked with methodical precision: cutting each tomato to identical size, measuring olive oil with a measuring spoon, setting a timer on his phone.

"You're timing tomatoes?" Maya asked, watching him.

"They need to roast evenly."

"They're tomatoes. They'll be fine."

"Even cooking is important for—" He stopped, looking at her dough situation. "Do you need help?"

Maya's dough had progressed from "too sticky" to "possibly correct" to "why is there flour everywhere, including in my hair?" She blew a strand off her forehead, leaving a white streak. "I'm good. This is the artistic process."

"That's one word for it."

"Says the man who just alphabetized the spice rack while I wasn't looking."

Derek had the grace to look slightly embarrassed. "They were disorganized."

"They were fine!"

"Fine is not optimal."

Chef Maria appeared at their station, surveying the scene: Maya covered in flour, Derek's precisely arranged mise en place, the contrast between their working styles. "How's it going, you two?"

"Great!" Maya said.

"We're managing different approaches," Derek said simultaneously.

Chef Maria smiled knowingly. "Pasta-making reveals a lot about a relationship. Some couples find it therapeutic. Others..." She looked pointedly at Maya's flour-covered apron, "...discover they have different definitions of 'enough flour.'"

After she moved on, Maya turned to Derek. "She thinks we're a disaster."

"We might be a disaster."

"Okay, but we're a *functional* disaster." Maya held up her dough, which had finally come together into a smooth ball. "See? Perfect."

Derek examined it critically. "It actually looks good."

"You sound surprised."

"I'm allowing for the possibility that chaos sometimes works." He checked his tomatoes, which were starting to blister and caramelize. "Though structure helps too. These are exactly where they need to be."

"Fine. Your tomatoes are perfect. My dough is perfect. We're both perfect. Now what?"

"Now you rest the dough for thirty minutes while I—" Derek checked his recipe card, "—prepare ingredients for the cream sauce. Which I can't actually cook until the pasta is ready."

"So we have thirty minutes of downtime."

"Apparently."

They stood there for a moment, the kitchen bustling around them. Other couples were at various stages—some working in seamless harmony, others bickering good-naturedly over chopped garlic sizes. At the station next to them, a couple was laughing as one of them accidentally knocked over a bowl of flour.

"Want to help me with my sauces?" Derek asked. "You could chop the garlic while I zest lemons."

Maya grabbed a knife. "I'm warning you, my chopping is not going to be uniform."

"I'm learning to accept that about you."

They worked side by side, Derek's methodical precision next to Maya's enthusiastic approximation. She told him about the sponsored post she was editing—a disaster involving a "sustainable" backpack that had split open in the middle of a market in Vietnam. He told her about a deal analysis at work that had required eighteen hours of revision because one decimal point was wrong.

"Eighteen hours for one decimal point?" Maya paused in her garlic chopping. "That's insane."

"That decimal point represented forty million dollars."

"Okay, that's fair. You win this round." She swept her very unevenly chopped garlic into a bowl. "But in my defense, if I mess up a caption, the worst that happens is some confused followers."

"Different stakes." Derek was zesting lemons with surgical precision, creating perfect little spirals. "Though your followers seem pretty invested. I saw the comments on your last post."

"You're reading my comments?"

"Research. Like I said." But Derek's ears were slightly pink, and he focused very intently on his lemon zesting.

Maya bumped his shoulder with hers. "You followed me back, by the way. I noticed."

"It seemed fair."

"Your Instagram is very... organized."

"Is that code for boring?"

"No! It's just—" Maya gestured with her knife, "—you post like, once a month. And it's always very composed. Nice photos, thoughtful captions. Mine is chaos."

"I noticed." Derek set down his zester, turned to face her. "But it's not boring chaos. It's... engaging. You make people feel like they're experiencing things with you."

Maya felt warmth spread through her chest that had nothing to do with the kitchen heat. "That's actually really nice of you to say."

"It's accurate." He paused. "Though you do use too many hashtags."

"Oh my god, take it back. The nice thing is canceled."

"I'm just saying, twelve hashtags per post is—"

"Strategic!" Maya pointed her knife at him, mock-threatening. "Hashtags are discoverability!"

"They're visual clutter."

"You sound like a designer."

"I appreciate clean aesthetics."

"You appreciate control."

"And you appreciate chaos."

They were standing very close now, both holding their respective tools like weapons in a very low-stakes standoff. Maya could see gold flecks in Derek's dark eyes behind his glasses, could see the exact moment his expression shifted from teasing to something else.

"Timer!" Derek's phone buzzed aggressively. He stepped back, checking it. "Tomatoes are done."

"Right. Tomatoes." Maya returned to her garlic, now somewhat mangled from her distracted chopping. "So what's next?"

The next thirty minutes were a study in contrasts. Derek's sauces came together with textbook precision—the tomatoes perfectly caramelized, the cream sauce smooth and properly emulsified. Maya's brown butter sage sauce involved one slightly burned batch ("That's not burned, that's deeply caramelized," she insisted), a near-disaster with boiling over, and ultimately, something that actually smelled incredible.

Rolling out the pasta was its own adventure. The Kitchen Collaborative had manual pasta machines at each station, and Maya approached hers with confident determination.

"Okay, so you just..." She fed her dough through the machine, which immediately stuck and bunched. "Huh."

"You need to flour it first," Derek said, appearing at her elbow with a small bowl of flour.

"I knew that."

"Did you?"

"I was about to do that." But Maya accepted the flour, dusted her dough, and tried again. This time it went through smoothly, creating a thin sheet. "Ha! Success!"

"Now you fold it and run it through again. Multiple passes, decreasing thickness each time."

"Are you reading the instructions?"

"I memorized them while the dough was resting."

"Of course you did." But Maya followed his guidance, and together they created long, thin sheets of pasta. Derek cut them into fettuccine with precise, even strokes. Maya's were less uniform but still respectable.

"Teamwork," she declared, holding up a handful of pasta strands.

"We haven't cooked them yet."

"Stop being a pessimist. We're killing this."

They weren't wrong. When Chef Maria made her final rounds, she stopped at their station and actually smiled with what looked like genuine approval.

"Well done, you two. Your sauces are properly balanced, your pasta is the right thickness, and you've managed to work together despite..." She gestured at their station, which looked like a flour bomb had detonated. "...your different approaches."

After she left, Derek and Maya plated their pasta, drizzling all three sauces artfully (Maya's word) or adequately (Derek's word) over the noodles. The final result looked restaurant-quality.

"We should take a picture," Maya said, pulling out her phone.

"For the content."

"For the content," she confirmed. But when she held up her phone to get the shot, Derek leaned in, and they both ended up in frame—flour-dusted, slightly sweaty from the kitchen heat, grinning over their shared creation.

"Good photo," Derek said, looking at her screen.

"Yeah." Maya stared at the image. They looked happy. More than that, they looked like a team. "Yeah, it really is."

They ate their pasta standing at their station, and Maya had to admit—grudgingly, silently—that it was the best thing she'd cooked in years. Maybe ever.

"This is really good," Derek said, surprise evident in his voice.

"You sound shocked."

"I thought with our different approaches, it would be..."

"A disaster?" Maya twirled more pasta on her fork. "We seem to be proving the algorithm right, despite our best efforts."

"It's one successful cooking class."

"Yeah, but we worked well together. Admit it."

Derek considered this, chewing thoughtfully. "We complemented each other. Your improvisation saved us when I was being too rigid about measurements. My timing kept your sauces from burning."

"So what you're saying is, I was right about us being a functional disaster."

"I'm saying..." Derek set down his fork, meeting her eyes, "...maybe the algorithm saw something we didn't."

Before Maya could respond, her phone buzzed. A notification from Synapse: Date #2 complete. Compatibility assessment: Increased to 98.1%. Next sync session will be scheduled within 96 hours.

She showed Derek her screen. "We went up."

"That's not—" He checked his own phone, saw the matching notification. "Huh."

"'Huh'? That's all you've got?"

"I don't know what it means."

"It means we're good at making pasta together."

"Or the algorithm is reading too much into collaboration."

Maya leaned against the counter, studying him. He'd relaxed over the course of the evening—tie loosened, sleeves pushed up, a small smudge of tomato sauce on his forearm that he hadn't noticed. He looked less like a financial analyst and more like a regular person. More like someone she could actually see herself spending time with.

Dangerous thought.

"So," she said, deflecting, "what did we learn tonight?"

"That you use way too much flour."

"Rude. What else?"

"That you tell stories while you cook. You narrated your entire sauce-making process like you were filming a tutorial."

"Occupational hazard." Maya bumped his shoulder. "What about you? What did you learn about yourself?"

Derek paused, considering seriously. "That maybe perfect technique isn't as important as perfect results. Your sauce was technically incorrect in about five ways, but it tasted great."

"Best compliment you've ever given me."

"It's only our second date."

"Fair point. You've got time to improve." Maya started untying her apron. "Walk me out?"

They cleaned their station together—Derek washing, Maya drying, a rhythm they fell into without discussion—and headed out into the cool Mountain View evening. Castro Street was busy with the dinner crowd, couples and friends heading to restaurants, tech workers in hoodies carrying to-go bags.

"My car's that way," Maya pointed left.

"I'm parked in the other direction."

They stood there for a moment, neither quite moving yet.

"This was fun," Maya said finally. "Unexpectedly fun."

"Yeah." Derek adjusted his glasses, a nervous tell she was starting to recognize. "Same time, same chaos next week?"

"Whenever the algorithm decides, apparently." Maya's phone buzzed—a text from Suzie demanding details. "I should go. But Derek?"

"Yeah?"

"Thanks for being a good partner tonight. Both in the kitchen and..." She gestured vaguely between them. "This whole weird experiment thing."

"Thanks for not burning down the kitchen."

"The night's still young. I might burn down my own kitchen later." But she was smiling as she said it, backing away toward her car. "See you soon, Chef Chen."

"See you, Chef Chaos."

Maya drove home with her phone playing her favorite playlist on shuffle, but she barely heard the music. She kept thinking about Derek's concentrated expression while he zested lemons, the way he'd stepped in to help without taking over, how they'd moved around each other in the kitchen space like they'd been doing it for years instead of hours.

Her phone buzzed at a stoplight. A text from Derek: *Made it to my car. Thanks again for tonight.*

Maya: *Coordinating safe arrivals now? Very on-brand*

Derek: *Just making sure you didn't get lost on the walk to your car*

Maya: *It was 100 feet!*

Derek: *You seem like someone who could get distracted in 100 feet*

Maya: *...fair*

When she got home, Suzie was waiting on the couch with wine and an expectant expression.

"Well?"

"We made pasta," Maya said, dropping onto the couch beside her.

"And?"

"And it was good. Really good. Both the pasta and the..." She gestured vaguely.

"The date?"

"Yeah. That." Maya accepted a glass of wine. "Suzie, I think I might be in trouble."

"Because you like him?"

"Because I wasn't supposed to like him. We were supposed to prove the algorithm wrong. We were supposed to be incompatible. But we made really good pasta together, and he made me laugh, and he's actually really thoughtful when he's not being annoyingly organized."

"So the algorithm might be right."

Maya took a long sip of wine. "That's the terrifying part."

Her phone buzzed again. She glanced at it, expecting another text from Derek, but it was an Instagram notification. He'd posted something—his first post in six weeks.

The photo was of their pasta dish, professionally composed (of course), with the caption:

> *Collaboration experiment: success. Sometimes opposing methods create the best results. #SynapseExperiment #PastaPartners*

Maya screenshot it immediately and texted him: *Did you just post on Instagram voluntarily?*

Derek: *Research purposes. Also, it was good pasta*

Maya: *You used TWO hashtags. I'm so proud*

Derek: *Don't get used to it*

Maya: *Too late. You're a content creator now. Welcome to the chaos.*

She posted her own photo—the one of both of them, flour-covered and grinning—with the caption:

> *Date #2: We made pasta and didn't kill each other. The algorithm is looking smug. Stay tuned. #SynapseExperiment #FunctionalDisaster #MaybeTheAIKnowsSomething*

The comments flooded in immediately:

> *@SuzieParksPhotography: You two are adorable and I will fight anyone who says otherwise*
> *@marcus_beats: My bro posted on IG. Hell has frozen over*
> *@wanderlust_adventures:THE CHEMISTRY THO*
> *@maya_superfan_01: I SHIP IT*

Maya put her phone face-down and looked at Suzie. "What am I doing?"

"I think," Suzie said gently, "you're letting yourself actually try. And that's terrifying because it's not your usual MO."

"My usual MO keeps me safe."

"Your usual MO keeps you lonely." Suzie squeezed her hand. "Maybe safe isn't what you need anymore.

Derek

Derek made it home by 9:15 PM, which was later than his usual weeknight routine, but he found he didn't mind. He'd enjoyed himself. More than enjoyed himself—he'd had actual, spontaneous fun, which wasn't something he could say about most of his evenings.

Marcus called as Derek was changing out of his flour-dusted clothes.

"Bro, you posted on Instagram."

"Hello to you too."

"No, seriously. You posted. With hashtags. Are you feeling okay? Should I call a doctor?"

Derek pulled on a t-shirt, shaking his head even though Marcus couldn't see him. "I made pasta. It seemed worth documenting."

"You made pasta with Maya."

"That's what couple's cooking classes involve, yes."

"And?" Marcus's voice was gleeful. "How was date number two?"

Derek sat on his bed, phone on speaker while he checked his notifications. The post had gotten more engagement in twenty minutes than his last three posts combined. People were commenting—mostly people he didn't know, probably Maya's followers finding his profile.

"It was good," he said finally. "We worked well together."

"That's it? 'Good'? 'Worked well together'? I'm your brother, man, give me something."

"What do you want me to say?"

"I want you to say whether you like her." Marcus paused. "Because you posted about her, which you never do. You didn't even post about Elena until you were engaged."

Derek lay back on his bed, staring at his ceiling. "She's... not what I expected."

"Good unexpected or bad unexpected?"

"Both." Derek tried to organize his thoughts. "She's chaotic and impulsive and uses way too much flour. But she's also thoughtful and funny and she makes me laugh in ways I don't usually laugh. And we made really good pasta together, which shouldn't matter but somehow does."

"Oh man, you're in deep."

"It's been two dates."

"Yeah, and you're already posting about her and analyzing your feelings. For you, that's basically engaged." Marcus's tone shifted, becoming more serious. "Look, I know Elena messed with your head. And I know you like things planned and certain. But maybe this—Maya, the algorithm, this whole experiment—maybe it's exactly what you need. Something you can't control or predict."

After they hung up, Derek opened Instagram again, scrolled through the comments on his post. People seemed excited about the "Synapse Experiment," about watching two seemingly incompatible people try to make it work. Some were rooting for them. Others were skeptical.

One comment stood out, from someone named @elena_volkov: Beautiful plating. Glad to see you're trying new things.

Elena had seen his post. Elena, who never commented on social media, who kept her online presence minimal and professional, had commented on his post about a date with someone else.

Derek stared at the comment for a long moment, then deliberately scrolled past it without responding.

He opened his texts instead, found his conversation with Maya, read through their exchanges from the evening. Her humor came through even in text—the way she'd teased him about coordinating safe arrivals, how she'd celebrated his two-hashtag post like he'd achieved something monumental.

He typed: *For the record, I had fun tonight*

Then deleted it.

Typed: *Thanks for being patient with my need to measure everything*

Deleted that too.

Finally settled on: *Same time next week feels too far away*

He sent it before he could overthink it.

Three dots appeared immediately, showing Maya was typing. Then disappeared. Then appeared again.

Finally: *Wow, Derek Chen admitting he wants to see me again. The algorithm is doing victory laps*

Derek: *The algorithm can be smug. It earned it*

Maya: *Did you just admit the algorithm might be right?*

Derek: *I'm admitting we make good pasta together. Everything else is still under review*

Maya: *Such a romantic*

Derek: *You knew what you were signing up for*

Maya: *Did I though?*

Derek smiled at his phone, then typed: *Maybe we're both figuring it out as we go*

Maya: *That's unexpectedly zen of you*

Derek: *Don't get used to it*

Maya: *Everyone keeps saying that to me tonight*

They texted for another twenty minutes about nothing important—her disastrous attempt at assembling furniture earlier that week, his ongoing battle with a coworker who kept stealing his labeled food from the office fridge. Easy conversation, the kind Derek rarely had with people outside his small circle.

When they finally said goodnight, Derek set his phone on his nightstand and realized something unsettling: his carefully maintained schedule for tomorrow—Friday, usually his catch-up day for any work that had slipped through the week—suddenly felt less important than it usually did.

He wanted to text Maya again, just to keep talking.

He wanted to skip ahead to date number three.

He wanted to know if she was thinking about him the way he was, frustratingly, thinking about her.

Instead, he opened his calendar and, for the first time in years, left Saturday completely blank. No plans, no structure, no color-coded blocks of predetermined activities.

Just empty space.

Just possibility.

5. Locked In

Derek

The notification came on Sunday afternoon while Derek was reviewing a pitch deck for a Monday meeting. His phone buzzed, and he found himself smiling before he even read it—a Pavlovian response he'd developed over the past few days.

> *SYNC SESSION #3 SCHEDULED*
> *Activity: Escape Room Challenge - "The Algorithm's Puzzle"*
> *Location: Cipher Escape Rooms - Middlefield Road*
> *Tuesday, 7:00 PM*
> *Note: This session tests problem-solving compatibility under pressure. Work together or fail together.*

Derek screenshot it and sent it to Maya: *Escape room. Tuesday. Thoughts?*

Her response was immediate: *OH HELL YES. I love escape rooms. Warning: I get VERY competitive*

Derek: *Competitive how?*

Maya: *Like, I once refused to speak to Suzie for three hours because she wouldn't let me try my idea and we ran out of time*

Derek: *That seems... intense*

Maya: *I contain multitudes. Also I'm really good at puzzles when people let me do my thing*

Derek: *I'm also good at puzzles when people follow logical approaches*

Maya: *Oh no*

Derek: *What?*

Maya: *We're going to fight, aren't we?*

Derek considered this. In escape rooms, he knew his tendency was to want to organize, strategize, create a systematic approach. Maya would want to just try things, trust her instincts, move fast. They'd clashed over flour measurements and cooking methods, but that had been lighthearted. This felt different—more potential for actual conflict.

Derek: *Probably. But we'll figure it out*

Maya: *Wow, optimism from Derek Chen. The algorithm is really doing its work*

Derek: *Or I'm learning that chaos isn't always bad*

Maya: *SCREENSHOT. SAVED. WILL USE AS EVIDENCE LATER*

Derek laughed out loud in his apartment, then immediately felt self-conscious about it even though no one was there to hear.

Tuesday evening, Derek arrived at Cipher Escape Rooms at 6:52 PM. The facility was in a strip mall, squeezed between a pho restaurant and a martial arts studio. Inside, the lobby was decorated with faux-ancient maps, mysterious symbols, and a leaderboard showing the fastest completion times for each room.

Maya rushed in at 6:58, slightly breathless, camera already in hand.

"Sorry, sorry—traffic on 101 was a nightmare." She was wearing black jeans and a vintage band t-shirt, hair in a high ponytail. "Have you checked in?"

"Yes. We're in room three—'The Algorithm's Puzzle.' Apparently, it's new, themed around AI and code-breaking."

"Of course the app put us in the AI-themed room. It's so meta it hurts." Maya signed the waiver the attendant handed her without reading it, which made Derek wince. "What? It's fine."

"You should read waivers before signing them."

"It's an escape room, not a skydiving expedition. What's the worst that could happen?"

A young guy with purple hair and a Cipher Escape Rooms polo appeared from a side door. "Maya and Derek? I'm Tyler, I'll be your game master tonight. Follow me."

He led them down a narrow hallway painted black, past doors labeled with different room themes: The Pharaoh's Tomb, The Haunted Asylum, The Heist. At the end of the hall, he stopped at a door marked with circuit board patterns and binary code.

"Okay, so 'The Algorithm's Puzzle' is our newest room, and it's tough. Only twelve percent of teams have escaped so far." Tyler was clearly excited about this statistic. "You've got sixty minutes. The goal is to find the master code that will unlock the final door. You'll need to solve a series of puzzles that will give you pieces of the code. Work together, think logically, but also trust your instincts. Questions?"

"Do we get hints?" Derek asked.

"Three hints maximum. I'll be monitoring from the control room. If you press the red button on the wall, I'll give you a clue via speaker." He pushed open the door. "Good luck. Your time starts when the door closes behind you."

They stepped into a room that looked like a high-tech laboratory mixed with a computer server room. Monitors lined one wall, showing cascading green code like something from The Matrix. A large whiteboard dominated another wall, covered in complex equations and symbols. There was a desk with a locked drawer, a filing cabinet, several colored boxes secured with different types of locks, and wires connecting various objects in patterns Derek couldn't immediately decipher.

The door shut behind them with an ominous click.

A timer on the wall began counting down: 60:00, 59:59, 59:58...

"Okay," Derek said, instinctively moving toward the whiteboard. "We should establish a systematic approach. I'll take the equations, you search for—"

But Maya was already across the room, pulling open unlocked drawers, lifting objects, checking under the desk. "There's a UV flashlight here—oh, and look, hidden messages on the wall!" She flicked on the flashlight, revealing glowing text previously invisible:

> *THE KEY TO UNDERSTANDING IS SEEING PATTERNS WHERE OTHERS SEE CHAOS.*

"That's a clue," Derek said, abandoning the whiteboard to join her. "Patterns in chaos. So we're looking for order in seeming randomness."

"Or we're overthinking it and it's just atmospheric text." Maya was already moving to the filing cabinet, trying to open it. "Locked. We need a key or a combination."

Derek returned to the whiteboard, studying the equations more carefully. They weren't random—he could see recurring numbers: 4, 7, 15, 23. "Maya, these numbers repeat. Four, seven, fifteen, twenty-three."

"Cool. What do they mean?"

"I don't know yet. Maybe they're part of a sequence?" He pulled out his phone to use the calculator.

"Wait, are you allowed to use your phone?"

"Tyler didn't say we couldn't."

"That feels like cheating."

"It's a tool. We're solving puzzles, not taking an exam." But Derek pocketed his phone anyway, not wanting to argue. "Fine. Let me think about it."

Maya had moved to the colored boxes—red, blue, green, yellow—each secured with a different lock type. "The red one has a four-digit combination lock. The blue one has a key lock. Green has a weird symbol lock, and yellow has..." She squinted. "Something I've never seen before."

"So we need to find four digits, a key, the meaning of symbols, and... whatever opens the yellow box." Derek felt his organizational instincts kicking in. "We should divide and conquer. You take the physical search, I'll work on the logic puzzles."

"Or we both do everything together so we don't miss connections."

"That's less efficient."

"But we might see things the other person doesn't." Maya turned to face him fully. "Derek, we're a team. The whole point is collaboration, remember? Like the pasta."

Derek took a breath, recognizing she was right even as his instinct was to optimize and systematize. "Okay. Together. What do you think we should tackle first?"

"The UV light revealed a message. Maybe there are more hidden things." Maya started methodically checking walls, furniture, even the ceiling with the UV flashlight. Derek joined her, and within minutes, they'd found three more hidden messages:

BINARY SPEAKS TRUTH
TIME IS RELATIVE
THE ANSWER IS IN THE QUESTION

"Okay, so binary..." Derek looked at the monitors showing cascading code. "That code on the screens isn't random. It's probably binary that translates to something."

"Can you read binary?"

"Not fluently, but I know the basics. Binary is base-two—each digit is either zero or one, and sequences of eight digits make up letters or numbers." He approached the nearest monitor, trying to capture a sequence before it scrolled away. "This is going to take forever to decode by hand."

"Wait." Maya pulled out her phone. "There are binary translator apps."

"I thought you said using phones was cheating."

"That was before I realized we have to decode an entire wall of binary. I'm practical, not proud." She downloaded an app, started photographing the screen. "Okay, let's see... this sequence translates to... '0417.'"

"Four, seventeen." Derek's mind raced. "Not four, seven, fifteen, twenty-three. Different numbers."

"Maybe they're coordinates? Or part of different codes?"

They spent the next fifteen minutes decoding binary, finding sequences that translated to: 0417, 1523, and 0847. Maya wrote them on the whiteboard in large numbers.

"Three sets of digits," she said. "And we have boxes that need codes. The red box needed four digits."

"Try zero-four-one-seven."

Maya spun the combination lock on the red box: 0-4-1-7. Click. The lock opened. Inside was a small brass key and a note:

> *CONGRATULATIONS. YOU'RE 20% THERE. THE KEY OPENS ONE PATH. CHOOSE WISELY.*

"The key could open the blue box or the filing cabinet," Derek said, analyzing their options. "We should determine which choice advances us further before we—"

Maya had already walked over to the blue box and inserted the key. It opened, revealing a complex puzzle made of sliding tiles with symbols on them.

"Maya!"

"What? We got the key, we used the key. That's how adventures work."

"But what if the key was supposed to open the filing cabinet? What if we just locked ourselves out of a necessary path?"

"Then we'll figure it out." She lifted the tile puzzle out of the box. "Look, it's one of those slide puzzles where you have to arrange symbols in order. I'm good at these."

Derek felt frustration building but forced himself to breathe. Different approaches. She was impulsive, he was cautious. The algorithm had said they'd need to work together.

"Okay," he said. "You work on that. I'm going to see if there are other ways to open the filing cabinet."

He returned to the desk, searching more thoroughly. In the back of an unlocked drawer, he found a small card with a riddle:

> *I SPEAK WITHOUT A MOUTH AND HEAR WITHOUT EARS. I HAVE NO BODY, BUT I COME ALIVE WITH WIND. WHAT AM I?*

"It's an echo," Derek said aloud.

"What?" Maya looked up from the tile puzzle, which she was solving with surprising speed.

"This riddle. The answer is an echo." Derek looked around the room. "So we need to find something related to echoes or sound."

He clapped his hands. The sound bounced strangely off one wall—the wall with the monitors. He approached it, pressing his ear against the surface. Hollow. There was a seam in the wallpaper, barely visible.

"Maya, there's something behind this wall."

She abandoned the puzzle, joining him. Together they found a hidden panel that pushed inward, revealing a small compartment containing a voice recorder and a note:

SPEAK THE PASSWORD: THE SUM OF ALL PATTERNS.

"The sum of all patterns," Maya repeated. "What patterns? The numbers on the whiteboard?"

Derek pulled out his mental calculator. "The recurring numbers were four, seven, fifteen, twenty-three. Sum is forty-nine. The binary numbers were zero-four-one-seven, fifteen-twenty-three, and zero-eight-four-seven." He did the math quickly. "Those sum to... eighty-seven total if we add all the individual digits, or they could be separate—"

"Just try forty-nine," Maya said. "Start simple."

Derek pressed the button on the voice recorder and spoke clearly: "Forty-nine."

A mechanical sound echoed through the room. The filing cabinet drawer popped open.

"Yes!" Maya high-fived him without thinking, and Derek found himself grinning back.

Inside the filing cabinet were multiple folders, each labeled with a different year: 2019, 2020, 2021, 2022, 2023. Maya grabbed them all, spreading them on the desk.

"Each folder has a single page with a date and a symbol," she said, laying them out. "March 4th, 2019—

triangle. July 15th, 2020—circle. November 23rd, 2021—square. April 17th, 2022—diamond. August 8th, 2023—star."

"Those dates..." Derek grabbed the whiteboard marker, writing them out. "March fourth is three-four. July fifteenth is seven-fifteen. November twenty-third is eleven-twenty-three."

"The recurring numbers!" Maya was bouncing slightly with excitement. "Four, seven, fifteen, twenty-three—they're from the dates!"

"And the symbols must correspond to the lock on the green box." Derek examined it—a lock with five symbol slots, and a dial with various shapes. "We need to enter them in order: triangle, circle, square, diamond, star."

Working together, they carefully input each symbol. The lock clicked open, and inside was a circuit board with wires connecting different numbered terminals.

"Oh no," Maya said. "I hate wire puzzles. I always cut the wrong one."

"This isn't about cutting. Look—" Derek pointed. "The wires connect numbers. Terminal one connects to terminal seven. Terminal four connects to terminal fifteen. It's showing relationships."

"More number patterns. I'm sensing a theme." Maya pulled out her phone, checking the timer. "We've got twenty-two minutes left. What about the yellow box? We still haven't opened it."

The yellow box's lock was bizarre—a series of rotating discs with letters on them that needed to align to form a word.

"It's a word lock," Derek said. "We need a password."

"All those clues we found—'The answer is in the question,' 'Time is relative,' 'Binary speaks truth'—maybe they spell something?"

They tried various combinations: TRUTH, TIME, QUESTION, ANSWER. Nothing worked.

Derek looked at the timer: 19:47, 19:46, 19:45...

"Wait," Maya said suddenly. "The clues aren't about what they say. They're about what they ARE. The key to understanding is seeing patterns where others see chaos—we found patterns in random numbers. Binary speaks truth—the binary code gave us real information. Time is relative—" She looked at the dates. "The dates weren't in chronological order in the folders, but we had to put them in order to solve it. The answer IS in the question!"

"What question?"

"The riddle! 'What am I?' The answer was ECHO." Maya started turning the discs on the yellow box: E-C-H-O-S.

Nothing.

"CODES?" Derek suggested.

Maya tried: C-O-D-E-S.

The yellow box clicked open.

Inside was a single sheet of paper with a message:

> *YOU'VE SOLVED THE PUZZLES. NOW SOLVE EACH OTHER.*
> *PARTNER A: Say what you fear most about this experiment.*
> *PARTNER B: Say what you hope for most from*

this experiment.
Speak honestly. The room is listening.

Maya and Derek looked at each other.

"Are you kidding me?" Maya laughed, but it sounded slightly nervous. "The escape room is doing couples therapy now?"

"Apparently." Derek adjusted his glasses. "This is what the algorithm's doing. 'The Algorithm's Puzzle'—it's not just about solving puzzles. It's about us."

"Sneaky AI." But Maya's smile had faded, and she looked genuinely uncertain. "So... who's Partner A and who's Partner B?"

"I'll go first," Derek said before he could overthink it. "I'll be Partner A."

Maya nodded, waiting.

The timer ticked: 16:32, 16:31, 16:30...

Derek took a breath. They were in an escape room, being watched by a game master, with a camera recording their every move, and he was supposed to be vulnerable? This was absurd. This was manipulative. This was—

"I'm afraid," he said quietly, "that I'll do everything right—follow all the rules, be present, try my best—and you'll still leave. Because that's what people do. They leave when the excitement wears off, or when something more interesting comes along, or when they realize that being stable and reliable is just code for boring."

The room was silent except for the soft hum of electronics and the clicking timer.

Maya's expression had shifted entirely, all humor gone. "Derek..."

"Your turn," he said. "What do you hope for?"

She took a visible breath, her hand unconsciously moving to her compass necklace. "I hope that for once—for once—I can stay. That I want to stay more than I want to run. That someone will make me feel like staying is the adventure, not the trap." Her voice cracked slightly. "I hope you prove me wrong about what I think I need to be happy."

The timer hit 15:00, and the final door—the one they'd assumed led to victory—clicked open with a mechanical sound.

But neither of them moved.

They stood in the center of the room, surrounded by solved puzzles and decoded messages, staring at each other while everything they'd just admitted hung in the air between them.

"Maya—" Derek started.

"We should get out," she said quickly, moving toward the open door. "We solved it. We won."

Derek followed her through the door into a small exit corridor that led back to the lobby. Tyler was waiting, grinning.

"Fifteen minutes, forty-two seconds! That's the third-fastest time for that room. You guys crushed it!" He was pulling up their photo—apparently, there had been a camera that caught their entry. "Want to post this on our social media wall of champions?"

"Sure," Maya said, but her voice was distant.

They collected their things, posed for the victory photo (Maya's smile looked forced, Derek noted), and stepped out into the parking lot. The sun had set while they were inside, and Mountain View's evening air was cool and sharp.

"That was intense," Derek said, unsure how to navigate what had just happened.

"Yeah." Maya was looking at her phone, not at him. "Really good problem-solving, though. We make a good team."

"Maya, about what I said in there—"

"It's fine." She finally looked up, but her expression was carefully neutral. "The room asked, we answered. That was the puzzle. We solved it."

"It wasn't just a puzzle." Derek stepped closer. "I meant what I said."

"I know." Her voice was soft. "That's what makes it scary."

His phone buzzed. A notification from Synapse:

> *Date #3 complete. Compatibility assessment: Increased to 98.4%. Warning: Emotional vulnerability detected. Integration phase beginning. Prepare for deeper connection in subsequent sessions.*

Derek showed Maya his screen. She read it, and something flickered across her face—fear, maybe, or longing, or both.

"The algorithm is getting creepy with its insights," she said, attempting lightness.

"Or it knows what it's doing."

"That's what I'm afraid of." She backed toward her car. "I should go. Early meeting tomorrow."

"Maya, wait—"

"Derek, I just—" She stopped, struggling with something. "I need to process. Tonight was a lot. Not just the escape room, but... everything. Can we just... take a beat?"

Every instinct Derek had was screaming at him to push, to process now, to not let this moment slip away. But he looked at her face—genuinely overwhelmed, needing space—and remembered her third condition from their first date: Life's too short to waste time on people who don't want to be there.

She wasn't saying she didn't want to be there. She was saying she needed time to figure out if she could let herself be there.

"Okay," Derek said. "Take your time."

"Yeah?" She looked relieved and disappointed simultaneously.

"Yeah. But Maya? For what it's worth—I'm not going anywhere. So whenever you're ready to process, I'm here."

She nodded, not trusting herself to speak, and got in her car.

Derek watched her drive away, then sat in his own car without starting it, replaying the last hour. They'd solved every puzzle in the room efficiently, working as a real team. And then the final puzzle had asked them to solve each other, and suddenly all their careful pretense about "proving the algorithm wrong" had crumbled.

Because they weren't proving it wrong.

They were proving it devastatingly, terrifyingly right.

Maya

Maya made it three blocks before she had to pull over.

Her hands were shaking on the steering wheel. Her heart was racing. She felt like she'd just jumped off another cliff, except this time she couldn't see the water below.

I'm afraid you'll still leave.

I hope you prove me wrong about what I think I need to be happy.

She'd meant to keep things light. She'd meant to document this experiment, prove the algorithm wrong, and walk away with great content and her independence intact. She hadn't meant to catch actual feelings for Derek Chen with his color-coded calendar and his earnest glasses-adjusting and his devastating honesty.

Her phone buzzed. Multiple texts:

> *Suzie: How was the escape room???*
>
> Marcus_beats (via Instagram DM)*: My brother just texted me "I told her I'm afraid she'll leave" and then stopped responding. WHAT HAPPENED*
>
> Derek: *Get home safe. No pressure to respond. Just want to know you're okay.*

Maya stared at that last message for a long moment.

She typed: *Home. Processing. You were right—that was more than just a puzzle*

Derek: *Yeah*

Maya: *I need some time but that doesn't mean I'm running*

Derek: *I'll be here*

Three words. Simple, direct, and somehow exactly what she needed to hear.

Maya drove the rest of the way home, where Suzie was waiting with the intensity of someone who'd been refreshing Instagram for updates.

"Spill," Suzie demanded the moment Maya walked in.

"We solved the escape room."

"And?"

"And the final puzzle made us say our fears and hopes about the experiment out loud, and Derek said he's afraid I'll leave because that's what people do, and I said I hope he proves me wrong about what I need to be happy, and then we just stood there having this MOMENT and it was supposed to be a fun date but instead it turned into emotional warfare—"

"Breathe," Suzie interrupted.

Maya took a breath.

"Okay," Suzie said. "So you both admitted you're scared because you're starting to care. That's good."

"How is that good? That's terrifying!"

"It's good because it's honest. May, you've spent years keeping things surface-level. The second a relationship started getting real, you'd find a reason to leave—a trip, a project, a convenient excuse. But Derek just told you he's afraid you'll do exactly that, and instead of running, you told him you hope you won't."

"What if I do run anyway? What if I can't help it?"

"What if you don't?" Suzie pulled her into a hug. "What if this is the one that finally makes you want to stay?"

Maya let herself be held, trying to slow her racing thoughts. Her phone buzzed in her pocket—probably more messages, more notifications, more people invested in this experiment. She'd turned her relationship into content, and now thousands of people were watching, waiting to see if the algorithm was right.

But that wasn't what scared her.

What scared her was that she wanted it to be right.

Derek

Derek made it home by 9:30 and immediately called Marcus, needing to talk to someone who knew him well enough to understand.

"What the hell happened?" Marcus answered without preamble.

"The escape room had a final puzzle that required emotional vulnerability."

"Only in Silicon Valley would an escape room force couples therapy." Marcus sounded simultaneously amused and concerned. "What did you say?"

Derek recounted the conversation, and Marcus was quiet for a long moment.

"Damn, bro. That's heavy."

"I know."

"But also really honest."

"I know."

"And she didn't run."

"Not yet." Derek sat on his couch, feeling exhausted. "But she might. She's processing, which is probably code for figuring out how to let me down easy."

"Or," Marcus said carefully, "she's actually processing. Because maybe this is hitting her as hard as it's hitting you."

Derek wanted to believe that. But his history—with Elena, with others before her—had taught him that when someone needed space to think, it usually meant they were preparing to leave.

"I shouldn't have said anything," Derek said. "It's only been three dates. This is too fast."

"Man, when has your life ever been fast? You dated Elena for three years before you proposed. You've been in the same apartment for five years. You've had the same gym routine for longer than some people have been adults. Maybe fast is exactly what you need."

After they hung up, Derek pulled up Maya's Instagram. She'd posted a photo from the escape room—the two of them in front of the victory board, her making a peace sign, him looking genuinely happy. The caption read:

> *Date #3: Escaped the room. Can't escape the feelings. The algorithm is playing for keeps. #SynapseExperiment #EmotionalPuzzles*

#MaybeImInTrouble

The comments were overwhelming:

@SuzieParksPhotography: YOU TWO
@wanderlust_adventures: This is the content I LIVE for
@marcus_beats: Proud of my boy for being brave
@elena_volkov: Hope you find what you're looking for

That last comment made Derek's chest tighten. Elena, watching from the periphery, bearing witness to him trying something real with someone else. He almost commented back, then decided against it. That chapter was closed. Derek opened his notes app and typed:

Three dates in, and I'm already breaking my own rules. I'm thinking about her when I should be working. I'm leaving space in my schedule that used to be sacred. I'm saying things I've never said to anyone, including Elena. The algorithm matched us at 97.8% compatible, and every date that number goes up. But compatibility isn't what scares me. What scares me is that I want this to work more than I've wanted anything in years, and I have no idea how to control that.

He saved it, labeled it "Maya—thoughts," and then closed his laptop before he could overthink any further.

His phone buzzed one more time. A message from Maya: *Thank you for giving me space. Most guys wouldn't*

Derek: *Most guys aren't me*

Maya: *I'm starting to notice that*

Derek smiled at his phone, and despite everything—the fear, the uncertainty, the vulnerability—he felt something he hadn't felt in years - Hope.

6. The Plumed Horse

Friday, 7:15 PM

Maya

Maya changed outfits four times before settling on a black dress that Suzie had insisted made her look "confident but not trying too hard." She'd been aiming for "I'm totally fine having dinner with my boyfriend's ex-fiancée" energy, which was apparently impossible to achieve through clothing alone.

"You look beautiful," Suzie said from the doorway, watching Maya apply lipstick with shaking hands. "And you're going to be fine."

"What if I'm not? What if I see them together and realize Derek's still in love with her? What if she's perfect and elegant and I spill something on myself in the first five minutes?"

"Then you'll handle it. Because you're Maya Reyes and you've talked your way out of worse situations." Suzie handed her a small clutch. "Phone, ID, credit card, emergency lip gloss. Everything you need."

"I need a time machine and a less complicated dating life."

"Too late. Derek's outside."

Maya looked out the window. Derek's car was parked in front, and he was leaning against it, checking his phone. He wore a dark suit—not quite formal, but definitely more dressed up than she'd ever seen him. He looked good. Really good. And terrified.

She grabbed her clutch and headed downstairs.

Derek looked up when she emerged, and his expression shifted from nervous to something else entirely. "Wow."

"Too much?"

"No. Perfect. You're perfect." He opened the car door for her. "Are you ready for this?"

"Absolutely not. You?"

"Not even a little bit." He got in the driver's side, started the engine, then just sat there for a moment. "Maya, if at any point tonight you want to leave—"

"I know. Same goes for you." She reached over, took his hand. "We're doing the hard thing together, remember?"

"Together," he repeated, like a promise.

They drove to Saratoga mostly in silence, both lost in their own thoughts. The Plumed Horse was one of those restaurants that looked expensive from the outside—understated elegance, soft lighting, the kind of place where people celebrated anniversaries and closed business deals.

"I've never been here," Maya said as they pulled into the parking lot.

"I have. Once. With Elena. For our engagement celebration."

Maya's stomach dropped. "Derek—"

"It's fine. It's just a restaurant." But his jaw was tight as he parked. "James chose it. He doesn't know the history."

They sat in the car for another moment, neither quite ready to go in.

"We could still leave," Maya offered. "Drive to In-N-Out, get burgers, pretend the algorithm never scheduled this."

"Tempting." Derek squeezed her hand. "But no. We're here. Let's do this."

Inside, The Plumed Horse was even more elegant than Maya had feared—all white tablecloths and crystal and the kind of quiet that made you feel like you should whisper. The host checked their reservation, then led them through the dining room to a table near the back.

James and Elena were already there.

James stood immediately, looking relieved to see them. "Hey! You made it. I was worried—well, you're here. That's great."

Elena remained seated but smiled warmly. She wore a cream-colored dress that probably cost more than Maya's entire wardrobe, and her hair was perfectly styled in a way that looked effortless but definitely wasn't.

"Maya, Derek, it's good to see you both," Elena said, her voice genuinely friendly.

"You too," Derek said, his voice carefully neutral.

Maya felt like she was watching this from outside her body as they all sat down—Derek pulling out her chair, James doing the same for Elena, everyone arranging themselves in this careful tableau of civilized adults having dinner together.

The seating arrangement was strategic, probably algorithm-designed: Derek and Maya on one side, James and

Elena on the other, forcing them all to look at each other throughout the meal.

"So," James said once they were settled, clearly trying to break the ice. "This is... a thing that's happening."

"Very much a thing," Maya agreed, accepting a menu from the server who'd materialized beside them. She scanned it quickly—everything was in French or Italian, prices weren't listed, portions were probably tiny. She was so out of her depth.

"The tasting menu is excellent," Elena offered. "If you like letting the chef choose."

"I prefer making my own decisions," Maya said, then immediately regretted how that sounded. "I mean—I like knowing what I'm eating. Surprises make me anxious."

Derek's hand found hers under the table, squeezed once.

A server appeared to take drink orders. Elena ordered wine with the kind of confidence that came from knowing exactly what she liked. James got a craft beer. Derek ordered his usual—whiskey, neat. Maya almost ordered her go-to vodka soda but found herself saying, "I'll have the same as him," nodding toward Derek.

The server left, and silence descended on the table.

"So," James tried again, "how have the other dates been going? Derek mentioned you guys did a cooking class?"

"Two cooking experiences, actually," Derek said. "The initial Synapse class, and then we went to the farmers market and cooked at my place."

"The farmers market wasn't algorithm-scheduled," Maya added, wanting Elena to know they'd chosen to spend time together. "Derek asked me on a non-Synapse date."

"That's great," Elena said, and she sounded like she meant it. "Derek never did spontaneous dates with me. It's nice to see him branching out."

The comment hung there—not malicious, but definitely loaded. Maya felt Derek tense beside her.

"People change," Derek said quietly. "Or maybe different people bring out different things."

"That's true," Elena agreed, looking at James. "James has me trying things I never would have before. We went rock climbing last weekend."

"You hate heights," Derek said before he could stop himself.

"I used to. Turns out I just hadn't found the right person to do it with." Elena's expression was gentle but firm. "Derek, I'm not saying what we had wasn't real. But it wasn't right. You know that."

"I do know that." Derek's voice was steady but Maya could feel the tension in his body. "It just took me a while to see it."

Their drinks arrived, providing a momentary reprieve. Maya took a sip of whiskey and immediately regretted it—it burned going down, tasted like lighter fluid, and she had to work very hard not to cough.

Derek noticed. "You didn't have to get what I got."

"I wanted to try it."

"It's an acquired taste."

"Everything about you is an acquired taste," Maya said, then froze. "That came out wrong."

But Derek was smiling—actually smiling. "No, that's accurate."

James laughed, some of the tension breaking. "Man, she's got your number."

"She really does," Derek agreed, looking at Maya with something warm in his eyes.

Elena was watching them with an unreadable expression. "You two are very different from how Derek and I were."

"How so?" Maya asked, not sure she wanted the answer.

"We were very... synchronized. Same industry, same interests, same life goals. We fit together easily." Elena paused. "But easy isn't always right. You two—you challenge each other. I can see it. And that's what Derek needed. What he needs."

"What about what you needed?" Maya heard herself ask.

Elena looked at James, something soft crossing her face. "I needed someone who sees me as more than a resume. Who makes me want to be spontaneous. Who—" She laughed slightly. "Who makes me want to go rock climbing even though I hate heights."

"The algorithm works in mysterious ways," James said, raising his beer. "To unexpected matches."

They all drank to that, even Maya with her terrible whiskey.

The server returned to take food orders. Elena and James both ordered the tasting menu. Derek ordered something complicated in French. Maya, feeling out of her depth and slightly defiant, ordered the most expensive steak on the menu even though she wasn't sure she could afford to split this bill.

After the server left, Elena leaned forward slightly. "Can I ask you both something? About the experiment?"

"Sure," Derek said cautiously.

"Do you think the algorithm is right? About you being compatible?"

Maya and Derek looked at each other. This was the question, wasn't it? The one they'd been dancing around for eight dates and countless conversations.

"Yes," Derek said first. "I think it's right. Maybe not for the reasons it thinks, but yes."

"What do you mean, not for the reasons it thinks?" James asked, genuinely curious.

"The algorithm probably matches based on data—personality metrics, communication styles, life goals. And Maya and I don't match on most of that data. But we match on something deeper. We—" Derek paused, choosing words carefully. "We make each other want to be better. Different. More complete."

Maya felt her throat tighten. She'd never heard Derek articulate it quite like that.

"What about you, Maya?" Elena asked gently. "Do you think it's right?"

This was it. The moment to be honest or deflect. Maya looked at Derek—at his carefully composed expression that she'd learned to read over the past weeks, at the way he was holding himself together in this restaurant where he'd celebrated his engagement to someone else, at the way he'd driven her here and held her hand and ordered whiskey he knew she'd hate but let her try anyway.

"I think," Maya said slowly, "that the algorithm saw something I couldn't see. That I needed someone who would make me want to stay still. And Derek—" She met his eyes. "Derek makes staying feel like the biggest adventure."

Derek's expression cracked, just slightly, into something vulnerable and real.

"That's beautiful," Elena said, and she meant it. "Derek, you found someone who sees you. Really sees you."

"So did you," Derek replied, nodding toward James.

"Yeah," James said, looking slightly embarrassed by the emotion at the table. "Yeah, I really did."

Their appetizers arrived—tiny, elegant portions that Maya tried not to photograph for Instagram even though the plating was incredible. They ate and talked, and slowly, impossibly, the conversation became almost natural. James told a story about a disastrous team-building exercise at Meta. Elena talked about her time in London. Derek explained a complex financial deal in terms that made even Maya interested. Maya described her worst travel disaster—the time she'd gotten food poisoning in Bali and had to be hospitalized.

"You still went back to Southeast Asia after that?" Elena asked, surprised.

"Three times," Maya said. "Bad experiences don't ruin places for me. They're just part of the story."

"That's a good philosophy," James said.

"It's how I try to live." Maya took another sip of whiskey, now slightly more tolerable. "Every disaster is just future content."

"Is that what this is?" Elena asked, not unkindly. "Content?"

Maya felt Derek tense beside her. This was the question Elena had really been asking—are you using Derek for your Instagram feed?

"No," Maya said firmly. "I mean, I post about the experiment. That's part of the deal. But Derek isn't content to me. He's—" She struggled to find words that wouldn't sound too revealing, too vulnerable. "He's the thing I'm scared to lose."

The table went quiet.

"Okay," Elena said softly. "Okay. I'm sorry I asked."

"It's a fair question." Maya forced herself to look at Elena directly. "You're protecting someone you care about. I get it. And for the record—I'm trying really hard not to mess this up."

"We both are," Derek added.

Their main courses arrived. Maya's steak was perfectly cooked, probably the best thing she'd ever eaten. Derek had ordered fish—something delicate and French that she stole a bite of when he offered. James and Elena shared their tasting menu portions, moving in sync in a way that spoke of growing intimacy.

Maya watched Derek watch them—watched him see Elena with someone else, happy, moved on. She couldn't read his expression.

"Excuse me," Derek said suddenly, standing. "Restroom."

He left before anyone could respond.

Maya gave him thirty seconds, then stood as well. "I'll be right back."

She found Derek in the hallway near the restrooms, leaning against the wall, breathing carefully.

"Hey," she said softly.

"I'm fine."

"You're not fine. That's okay."

Derek looked at her, and she saw it—all the control he'd been maintaining, cracking. "This is harder than I thought it would be."

"Seeing her happy with James?"

"Seeing her be the person she never was with me." Derek's voice was tight. "She went rock climbing, Maya. She hates heights. I suggested it once when we were together, and she said it was dangerous and pointless. But James suggests it, and suddenly she's trying new things."

"Derek—"

"I know. I know it's not about me. I know we weren't right together. But it still—" He stopped, shook his head. "It still makes me wonder if I was the problem. If I was too boring, too predictable, too—"

Maya grabbed his face with both hands, making him look at her. "Stop. You are not boring. You are not the problem. Elena needed someone different, and you needed someone different, and that's okay. That's not a failure."

"Then why does it feel like one?"

"Because you're human. Because seeing your ex happy without you is hard even when you're happy without them." She softened her grip, stroking his jaw with her thumbs. "But Derek, you're here with me. And I went rock climbing in Vietnam and I'd do it again with you if you wanted. Not because you're James, but because you're you."

"I don't want to go rock climbing."

"Then we won't. We'll do Derek things and Maya things and whatever weird hybrid things we create together." She leaned up, kissed him softly. "But right now, we're going back to that table, and we're finishing this dinner, and we're showing the algorithm that we can handle complicated."

Derek kissed her back, deeper this time, his hands finding her waist. When they pulled apart, he was breathing harder but looked more settled.

"Okay," he said. "Okay. Let's do this."

They returned to the table, where James and Elena were pretending they hadn't noticed the absence.

"Everything okay?" James asked.

"Yeah," Derek said, sitting down and immediately taking Maya's hand on top of the table, not hiding it. "Everything's good."

The rest of dinner was easier. They talked about work, about the algorithm, about whether AI dating was the future or a dystopian nightmare. Elena and Maya even bonded slightly over difficult family expectations—Elena's traditional Russian parents, Maya's traditional Filipino family, both sets convinced their daughters were making questionable life choices.

"My mother still asks when I'm getting a real job," Maya admitted. "She doesn't understand that content creation is a real job."

"My parents don't understand why I left a good position in London to come back to the Bay Area," Elena said. "They thought I was running away."

"Were you?" Derek asked quietly.

Elena looked at him, then at James. "Maybe. But sometimes running away from the wrong thing leads you to the right thing."

Dessert arrived—elaborate constructions of chocolate and fruit and things Maya couldn't identify but tasted incredible. She photographed it instinctively, then caught herself.

"Sorry, work habit," she said.

"Post it," Elena encouraged. "The plating is beautiful."

"Yeah?" Maya looked at Derek, who nodded. She posted it quickly to her Instagram story:

> *Date #8: Facing fears and eating incredible dessert. The algorithm knows what it's doing. #SynapseExperiment*

James checked his phone, saw the story, showed Elena. They both liked it immediately.

"You have an amazing following," Elena said, scrolling through Maya's feed. "These travel photos are stunning."

"Thanks. It's my life's work. Literally." Maya took another bite of dessert. "What about you? What's your passion project?"

"Honestly? I'm trying to figure that out." Elena set down her fork. "I've spent so long optimizing my career that I forgot to think about what actually makes me happy. James is helping me figure that out."

"She's learning guitar," James said proudly. "Badly, but enthusiastically."

"Very badly," Elena confirmed, laughing. "But I'm trying. That's new for me."

The server brought the check, and there was a brief awkward moment when everyone reached for it. James got there first.

"We've got this," he said firmly. "You can get the next one."

"Next one?" Maya asked.

"If you'll have us," Elena said. "I know tonight was probably uncomfortable, but I'd like to do it again. Maybe somewhere less loaded with history next time."

Derek looked at Maya, silently asking. She thought about it—about Elena's genuine warmth, about James's obvious love for his best friend, about how much easier the night had gotten once everyone stopped pretending.

"Yeah," Maya said. "I'd like that."

"Me too," Derek added.

They walked out together, the four of them, into the cool Saratoga night. James and Elena headed toward James's car, but Elena turned back.

"Derek?" she called.

He stopped. "Yeah?"

"I'm really happy for you. Both of you." She meant it. "Don't let fear mess this up."

"I won't," Derek promised.

After they drove away, Derek and Maya stood by his car for a moment, neither quite ready to leave.

"That was intense," Maya said.

"That was the understatement of the year." Derek pulled her close. "Thank you for being here. For not running."

"Thank you for not letting her scare me off." Maya buried her face in his chest. "Derek, when she said we challenge each other—she's right. You challenge me to stay. To build something. To stop running."

"And you challenge me to let go. To be spontaneous. To stop controlling everything." He kissed the top of her head. "The algorithm really did know what it was doing."

Maya's phone buzzed. She pulled it out to see a Synapse notification:

> *SYNC SESSION #8 COMPLETE*
> *Compatibility Assessment: 98.9%*
> *Major milestone achieved: Relationship resilience confirmed in complex social dynamics*
> *Note: You have successfully navigated external*

> *pressure. Remaining sessions will test internal vulnerabilities. Prepare for deeper integration.*
>
> *Warning: Upcoming challenge will test core relationship assumptions. Trust your connection.*

Maya showed Derek the screen. He read it, frowning.

"'Test core relationship assumptions'? What does that mean?"

"I don't know. But it doesn't sound fun."

"Nothing with this algorithm has been easy."

"But it's been worth it." Maya looked up at him. "Right?"

"Yeah," Derek said, no hesitation. "It's been worth it."

They drove back to Mountain View, hands clasped between them, both wondering what challenge could possibly be harder than the one they'd just survived.

Maya

It was 11:30 PM when Derek dropped Maya off at her house. She was exhausted—emotionally wrung out from the dinner, from keeping her composure, from watching Derek process seeing his ex-fiancée happy with someone else.

Suzie was waiting up, of course.

"How bad?" she asked immediately.

"Not as bad as I feared. But also worse in ways I didn't expect." Maya collapsed on the couch. "Elena is genuinely nice. Like, frustratingly nice. And she and James are actually good together. And Derek handled it like an adult but I could see it hurting him."

"But you guys made it through."

"We made it through." Maya pulled out her phone, showing Suzie the final Synapse notification. "But apparently there's another challenge coming. Something about testing core relationship assumptions."

"You've faced the ex. What's left?"

"I don't know. That's what scares me."

Her phone buzzed. A text from Derek: Thank you for tonight. For being you. For staying.

Maya felt her chest tighten. She typed back: Thank you for making me want to stay

Then, before she could stop herself: *I think I'm falling in love with you*

She stared at the message for a long moment, cursor hovering over send.

"Don't overthink it," Suzie said, reading over her shoulder. "If you feel it, say it."

"What if it's too soon?"

"What if it's exactly the right time?"

Maya closed her eyes and hit send.

Three dots appeared immediately, showing Derek typing. Then disappeared. Then appeared again.

Finally: *I know I'm falling in love with you*

Maya's breath caught. She read the message three times, making sure she hadn't misunderstood.

Maya: *Yeah?*

Derek: *Since the pasta, probably. Maybe before. Definitely after tonight.*

Maya: *That's very specific for someone who's falling*

Derek: *I'm me. I track everything. Including feelings for you*

Maya laughed, crying slightly, feeling something huge and terrifying and wonderful expanding in her chest.

Maya: *We're doing this? Actually doing this?*

Derek: *I'm all in if you are*

Maya: *I'm all in*

Derek: *Good. Sleep well. I'll see you tomorrow*

Maya: *Tomorrow isn't a scheduled date*

Derek: *I know. I'm choosing to see you anyway*

Maya: *Derek Chen, rule breaker. I'm so proud*

After she said goodnight to Suzie and got ready for bed, Maya lay in the dark, staring at her ceiling, processing everything. She'd gone to dinner expecting disaster. She'd survived. More than survived—she'd stayed, she'd fought for what she and Derek had, and she'd told him she was falling in love.

And he'd said it back.

Her phone lit up one more time. A notification from Instagram—someone had commented on her dessert story. She opened it out of habit.

The comment was from an account she didn't recognize:

@synapse_official

We know what you need better than you know yourself. Trust the process. The next test begins soon.

Maya stared at the comment, a chill running through her. The algorithm had an Instagram account. The algorithm was commenting on her personal posts.

The algorithm was watching.

She screenshot the comment and sent it to Derek: *This is creepy right?*

Derek: *Very creepy. But also very Synapse*

Maya: *What do you think the next test is?*

Derek: *I don't know. But whatever it is, we'll handle it. Together*

Maya: *Together*

She put her phone on her nightstand, pulled her blanket up, and tried to sleep. But the algorithm's words kept echoing in her mind:

The next test begins soon.

Trust the process.

We know what you need better than you know yourself.

Derek

Derek lay in his own bed, staring at his own ceiling, replaying the entire night. Seeing Elena happy. Watching James with her, doing things Derek had never done. Realizing that his relationship with Elena had been comfortable but not right. Understanding, finally, that her leaving had been the best thing for both of them.

And then Maya—grabbing his face in that hallway, telling him he wasn't boring, kissing him like she meant it. Maya telling him she was falling in love with him.

Maya staying.

His phone buzzed. A message from James: *Thanks for tonight. I know it was weird. You're a good friend*

Derek typed back: *Thanks for being honest about the match. And for making her happy*

James*: You're really okay with this?*

Derek*: I'm getting there. Ask me again in a month*

James*: Fair. Also - Maya's great. Don't screw it up*

Derek*: Trying not to*

He was about to put his phone away when another notification came through. Email this time, from an address he didn't recognize:

algorithm_insights@synapse-ai.com

Subject: Relationship Assessment Update - Action Required

Derek opened it.

Dear Derek Chen,

Congratulations on successfully completing Sync Session #8. Your relationship with Maya Reyes has shown remarkable resilience under external pressure.

However, our algorithms have detected a potential compatibility anomaly that requires your attention. As part of our commitment to transparency and user satisfaction, we must inform you of a technical issue that may have affected your initial match.

On the night of your pairing (March 15th, 11:47 PM PST), our servers experienced a brief synchronization error during the matching process. While we have no reason to believe this affected the validity of your match, we cannot confirm with 100% certainty that your 97.8% compatibility score was calculated correctly.

We are conducting a full audit of matches created during this timeframe. Results will be available within 72 hours.

This notification is being sent out of an abundance of caution. Most matches from this period have been verified as accurate. However, we believe in radical transparency with our users.

Please do not be alarmed. Continue your relationship as normal. We will update you with our findings.

If you have questions, please contact our support team.

Best regards,
The Synapse Team

Derek read the email three times, his heart rate increasing with each pass.

A synchronization error.

His match with Maya might not be accurate.

The 97.8% compatibility that had seemed so certain, so validated by every date, every conversation, every moment—might be wrong.

He should tell Maya immediately. That would be the honest thing to do. The right thing to do.

But what if it scared her? What if she used it as an excuse to run?

What if the error was real, and everything they'd built was based on a mistake?

Derek's phone buzzed again. A text from Maya: *Still awake?*

He stared at the message, the email still open on his screen, torn between honesty and protection.

Derek: *Yeah. Just thinking*

Maya: *About tonight?*

Derek: *About everything*

Maya: *Good everything or scary everything?*

Both, Derek thought. Everything is both.

Derek: *Good. Definitely good. Get some sleep*

Maya: *You too. Love you*

She'd said it casually, like it was easy. Like it was true.

Derek typed back: *Love you too*

And he meant it.

But as he closed his eyes, the email haunted him: *We cannot confirm with 100% certainty that your compatibility score was calculated correctly.*

He would tell her. He would.

Just... not tonight.

Not when they'd just survived Elena and James.

Not when they'd just said "I love you."

He'd tell her tomorrow.

Or the day after.

Soon.

He'd tell her soon.

***

7. The Error Report

Saturday Morning - 18 Hours After The Email

Derek

Derek had slept maybe two hours. He'd spent most of the night staring at the ceiling, phone on his nightstand, the email from Synapse burning a hole in his consciousness.

We cannot confirm with 100% certainty that your compatibility score was calculated correctly.

At 3 AM, he'd almost called Maya. At 4 AM, he'd drafted a text explaining everything, then deleted it. At 5 AM, he'd given up on sleep and gone for a run, pushing himself harder than usual, trying to outrun the anxiety.

It didn't work.

Now, at 8:30 AM, he was sitting in his pristine kitchen with cold coffee and a problem he didn't know how to solve. The logical part of his brain—the analyst, the financial risk assessor—knew exactly what to do: tell Maya immediately, be transparent, deal with the consequences together.

But the other part—the part that had watched her almost run after the escape room, that had seen her fear when Elena challenged her commitment, that knew how easily she could convince herself to leave—that part said: *Wait. Make sure the error is real before you scare her.*

His phone buzzed. Maya: Good morning *Coffee later?*

Derek stared at the heart emoji. She never used emojis. This was new. This was her trying.

Derek: *My place or yours?*

Maya: *Yours. I want to see if you've cleaned up from our cooking disaster*

Derek: *It was cleaned up within an hour of you leaving*

Maya: *Of course it was. See you at 10?*

Derek: *Perfect*

He had ninety minutes to decide what to do.

Maya

Maya arrived at Derek's apartment at 10:07 with pastries from a French bakery on Castro Street and a lightness in her chest she wasn't used to. She'd woken up thinking about last night—about saying "I love you," about Derek saying it back, about surviving the dinner with Elena and coming out stronger.

She felt good. Actually, genuinely good.

Derek opened the door, and her smile faltered slightly. He looked tired—shadows under his eyes, hair not quite as perfectly arranged as usual, wearing sweatpants and a faded Stanford shirt instead of his usual put-together casual.

"Hey," she said, studying his face. "Did you sleep?"

"Some." He took the pastry bag from her, kissed her cheek, but something was off. His kiss was distracted. "Coffee's ready."

Maya followed him into the kitchen, watching him move. He was being careful—too careful. The way he poured her coffee, the way he arranged pastries on plates, the way he wouldn't quite meet her eyes.

"Derek, what's wrong?"

"Nothing's wrong."

"You're lying. You do this thing with your jaw when you're stressed—you clench it just slightly. And you're doing it right now." She set down her coffee cup. "What happened?"

"Nothing happened. I'm just tired from last night."

"Bullshit." Maya moved closer. "We survived dinner with your ex-fiancée. We said 'I love you.' Everything was good when we said goodnight. What changed between then and now?"

Derek's phone buzzed on the counter. He glanced at it, and something flickered across his face—guilt, maybe, or fear.

"Who's texting you?" Maya asked, hating how suspicious she sounded.

"No one. Just work."

"On a Saturday morning?"

"Maya, it's nothing—"

"Show me."

The words came out harder than she'd intended. Derek looked at her, something wounded in his expression.

"You don't trust me?"

"I trust you. I just know when you're hiding something." Her heart was starting to race, old fears surfacing. "Are you having second thoughts? About us? About last night?"

"What? No. Maya, no." He reached for her hand, but she pulled back.

"Then what is it? Because you're acting weird, and after everything we've been through, I need you to be honest with me."

Derek was quiet for a long moment, his jaw working, clearly having some kind of internal battle. Finally, he picked up his phone, pulled up an email, and handed it to her without a word.

Maya read it once, then again, her stomach dropping with each pass.

Synchronization error.

Cannot confirm with 100% certainty.

Compatibility score may not be accurate.

She looked up at him, feeling like the floor had disappeared beneath her feet.

"When did you get this?"

"Last night. After I dropped you off."

"Last night." Maya's voice was flat. "So when I texted you, when I said 'I love you,' you already knew about this."

"Maya—"

"And you didn't tell me." She set his phone down carefully, trying to keep her hands from shaking. "You let me say 'I love you,' you said it back, and you knew the entire time that our match might be a mistake."

"It's not a mistake—"

"You don't know that! The email says they can't confirm—"

"The email is covering their ass legally. It doesn't mean anything." Derek ran his hand through his hair, frustration breaking through. "Maya, we've had eight dates. We know each other. A potential glitch in the algorithm doesn't change what we have."

"Doesn't it?" Maya felt herself pulling back, that familiar urge to run rising in her chest. "Derek, we met because an algorithm said we were 97.8% compatible. We trusted that. We built everything on that foundation. And now you're telling me the foundation might be cracked?"

"No, I'm telling you that I got a scary email from a company covering their legal bases, and I didn't want to freak you out before we knew if it was even real."

"That's not your decision to make!" Maya's voice rose. "You don't get to decide what information I can handle. That's not protecting me, that's controlling me."

"I wasn't trying to control you—"

"Then what were you trying to do?"

Derek was quiet for a moment, and when he spoke, his voice was raw. "I was trying not to lose you. I saw your face after the escape room, after Elena challenged you, after every moment where you almost ran. And I thought—if I tell you about this error, if I give you a reason to doubt us, you'll convince yourself it's a sign. You'll leave. And I—" His voice cracked slightly. "I couldn't risk that. Not after last night. Not after you said you loved me."

Maya felt tears burning her eyes. "So you lied."

"I didn't lie. I just didn't tell you yet."

"That's the same thing, Derek." She grabbed her bag, needing to move, needing space. "I've been in relationships with people who decided what I could handle, who kept things from me 'for my own good.' I left those people. I won't do it again."

"Maya, please—" Derek stepped toward her. "Can we just talk about this? Can we figure it out together?"

"Together would have been telling me last night. Together would have been trusting me to handle it." She was at the door now, hand on the knob. "I need to think."

"Don't run." Derek's voice was quiet, desperate. "Please. That's what you do—something gets hard and you run. Don't do it this time."

Maya turned back, anger flashing. "You know what, you're right. I do run. It's my thing. But you want to know why? Because people always, always prove that staying is worse than leaving. They lie, they hide things, they decide what I get to know about my own relationship." She opened the door. "You had one job, Derek. Be honest. That was literally the only thing I asked for. And you couldn't do it."

"Maya—"

"I'll text you when I'm ready to talk. Or not. I don't know yet."

She left, closing the door firmly behind her, and made it to her car before the tears started.

Derek

Derek stood in his apartment, staring at the closed door, feeling like he'd just watched something precious shatter in slow motion.

His phone buzzed. A text from Marcus: *Bro, what happened? Maya just posted an Instagram story that says "When the algorithm glitches, so does your heart" with a crying emoji. WHAT DID YOU DO?*

Derek opened Instagram with shaking hands. Maya's story was up—a photo of the Synapse app icon with that caption. Already, comments were flooding in:

> *@SuziePar ksPhotography: May, call me*
>
> *@wanderlust_adventures: Oh no, what happened??*
>
> *@maya_superfan_01: NOOO NOT THE ALGORITHM ERROR*
>
> *@synapse_official: We're working on resolving any technical issues. Please contact support for individual concerns.*

Derek closed Instagram, feeling sick. She'd made it public. Their relationship crisis was now content for her followers.

He called James.

"Hey man, what's—"

"I messed up." Derek sat on his couch, head in his hands. "I got an email from Synapse saying there might have been an error in our matching algorithm, and I didn't tell Maya right away, and she found out, and she left, and I don't know how to fix this."

"Wait, slow down. There was an error? Like, you and Maya aren't actually compatible?"

"I don't know. The email was vague. But I should have told her immediately, and instead I waited because I was scared she'd use it as an excuse to leave, and now she's left anyway because I wasn't honest."

James was quiet for a moment. "Derek, man, I say this with love: what were you thinking?"

"I wasn't. I was just—" Derek exhaled roughly. "I was trying to protect what we have. She's always looking for reasons to run, and I didn't want to give her one."

"But by not telling her, you gave her a bigger reason."

"I know." Derek's voice was hollow. "I know that now."

"So what are you going to do?"

"I don't know. Give her space? Go after her? I don't—I don't know the right answer."

"The right answer is probably somewhere in the middle. Give her a little space to process, but don't let her completely disappear." James paused. "Also, you should probably figure out if the error is real. Because if it is, you guys need to decide if what you have is real regardless of what the algorithm says."

After hanging up, Derek opened his laptop and composed an email to Synapse support:

Dear Synapse Team,

I received an error notification regarding my match with Maya Reyes (Match #2847). I need to know:

1. What specifically was the synchronization error? 2. How does this affect our compatibility score? 3. When will the audit be complete? 4. If the score was wrong, what is the correct score?

This is urgent. My relationship depends on having accurate information.

Derek Chen

He sent it, then sat back, staring at his immaculately organized apartment—everything in its place, everything controlled, everything except the one thing that actually mattered.

His phone buzzed. A text from Maya: *I'm at Suzie's. I need time to think. Please don't call.*

Derek: *I understand. But Maya, I love you. That's not algorithm-dependent. That's real.*

Three dots appeared, showing she was typing. Then disappeared. Then appeared again. Finally:

Maya: *I need to figure out if I believe that.*

Maya

Maya was curled up on Suzie's couch, having cried through most of her mascara and half a box of tissues. Suzie sat beside her, rubbing her back, letting her process.

"Tell me again why you're so mad," Suzie said gently.

"Because he lied."

"He omitted information. That's different."

"It's the same thing!" Maya sat up, wiping her eyes. "Suzie, I told him honesty was my only real condition. The only one that mattered. And he couldn't do it."

"Because he was scared." Suzie handed her another tissue. "May, I'm not defending what he did. But I understand why he did it. He saw you almost run after the escape room. He watched you struggle through dinner with Elena. He knows your pattern. And he got an email that could have triggered that pattern, so he panicked."

"So it's my fault? Because I have commitment issues?"

"That's not what I'm saying." Suzie took Maya's hands. "I'm saying that Derek made a mistake because he was trying to protect something precious. That doesn't make it right, but it makes it human. And if you leave over this—if you use the algorithm error as your excuse to run—you're proving him right."

Maya pulled her hands away. "So I should just forgive him? Just forget that he kept something huge from me?"

"No. You should be mad. You should tell him exactly how this made you feel. But then you should ask yourself: is this a dealbreaker? Is one mistake, made out of fear, enough to throw away everything you've built?"

Maya's phone had been buzzing constantly—Instagram notifications, texts from people who'd seen her story. She'd turned it face-down, not ready to deal with the public aspect of this mess.

But now she picked it up, scrolled through the messages:

Marcus_beats (Instagram DM): *My brother is an idiot but he loves you. Please don't give up on him*

Elena_volkov (Instagram DM): *I saw your story. For what it's worth, Derek is terrible at relationships but excellent at trying. Give him a chance to fix this.*

James: *Derek's a mess. He knows he screwed up. He's not asking for forgiveness yet, just a chance to explain properly.*

And from Derek himself, a text that had come in while she was crying:

Derek: *I know I don't deserve a response. But I need you to know: the algorithm might have made a mistake, but I didn't. Choosing you, falling in love with you—that was all me. No algorithm required.*

Maya read it three times, feeling her anger soften slightly around the edges.

"What do I do?" she asked Suzie.

"What do you want to do?"

"I want to run. I want to book a flight somewhere and not think about this."

"But?"

"But." Maya took a shaky breath. "But I also want to stay. I want to fight for this. I want to believe that what we have is real even if the algorithm was wrong."

"Then do that."

"But what if the algorithm was the only reason we worked? What if we're not actually compatible and we've just been fooling ourselves?"

"Maya, listen to me." Suzie gripped her shoulders. "You and Derek worked because you chose to work. Every date, every conversation, every moment where you could have walked away and didn't—that was you two, not the algorithm. The algorithm just gave you permission to try."

Maya's phone buzzed again. An email notification. She opened it without thinking.

It was from Synapse:

Subject: Compatibility Audit Results - Match #2847

Her heart stopped. She opened it with shaking hands.

Dear Maya Reyes,

Thank you for your patience during our compatibility audit process. We have completed our review of Match #2847 (Maya Reyes & Derek Chen).

Our findings:

There was indeed a synchronization error on March 15th, 11:47 PM PST, affecting the initial compatibility calculation. Your original match score of 97.8% was calculated using incomplete data from Derek's profile due to a server timeout during the matching process.

After completing the full analysis with all available data, your corrected compatibility score is: 71.3%

This represents a significant discrepancy from the original score. According to our algorithm:

- Scores above 95% indicate exceptional long-term compatibility - Scores between 85-95% indicate strong compatibility with manageable differences

- Scores between 70-85% indicate moderate compatibility requiring significant compromise - Scores below 70% indicate fundamental incompatibility

Your corrected score of 71.3% suggests that while you share some compatible traits, your fundamental differences (spontaneity vs. structure, adventure-seeking vs. stability-preferring, independence vs. partnership orientation) may create long-term challenges.

We sincerely apologize for this error. As compensation, we are offering:

1. Full refund of all subscription fees 2. Six months of free premium service for future matching 3. Access to our relationship counseling services

You are under no obligation to continue this relationship. However, if you choose to proceed despite the lower compatibility score, we recommend professional relationship support.

Again, we apologize for any confusion or distress this error may have caused.

Sincerely,
Dr. Michelle Torres
Founder & CEO, Synapse AI

Maya read it once. Twice. Three times.

71.3%.

Not 97.8%.

71.3%.

Below the threshold for fundamental compatibility.

"Oh my god," she whispered.

"What?" Suzie looked over her shoulder, read the email, and swore softly. "Oh, May."

Maya's hands were shaking. "We're not compatible. The algorithm says we're not compatible. We're below—we're fundamentally incompatible."

"That's one algorithm's opinion—"

"An algorithm that correctly matched Elena and James. An algorithm that's been right about everything else." Maya stood up, pacing. "Derek was right. The foundation was cracked. And I—" She laughed, a slightly hysterical sound. "I yelled at him for not telling me, and it turns out the error is real and we're a mistake."

"You are not a mistake," Suzie said firmly. "Maya, you're letting a computer program tell you what you feel. That's insane."

"Is it? We met because of the algorithm. We trusted it. We built everything on that trust. And now it's saying we got it wrong."

Her phone rang. Derek. She stared at it, not answering.

It went to voicemail. Immediately rang again.

"You should answer," Suzie said.

"And say what? 'Hey, so that error was real and we're 71% compatible which means we're basically doomed'?"

"Or you could say 'I love you and numbers don't change that.'"

Maya looked at her phone, Derek's name still flashing. Her finger hovered over the answer button.

She let it go to voicemail.

Seconds later, a text: *Did you get the email from Synapse?*

Maya: *Yes*

Derek: *Can we talk? Please?*

Maya stared at the message, her mind racing. 71.3%. Fundamental incompatibility. Long-term challenges.

Everything they'd built—was it real? Or had they just been performing a compatibility that never actually existed?

Maya: *I don't know what to say*

Derek: *Then just listen. Please. Give me 10 minutes. In person. I'll come to you, you come to me, wherever you want. Just 10 minutes.*

Maya looked at Suzie, who nodded encouragingly.

Maya: *Shoreline Park. The amphitheater. 30 minutes*

Derek: *I'll be there*

"I don't know if I can do this," Maya said, already grabbing her bag.

"Yes you can. Because you're braver than you think." Suzie hugged her. "And because Derek is worth fighting for. And so are you."

Derek

Derek drove to Shoreline Park going exactly the speed limit but wanting to floor it. His mind was racing through every possible conversation, every way this could go.

He'd gotten the email from Synapse too. Seen the 71.3%. Felt his stomach drop.

But he'd also felt something else: certainty.

Because the number didn't change anything. Not for him.

He parked and walked to the amphitheater, where Maya was already waiting, sitting on the steps, looking small and scared and beautiful. When she saw him, she stood up, arms crossed defensively.

"Hi," Derek said.

"Hi."

They stood there for a moment, the awkwardness thick between them.

"You got the email," Derek said.

"71.3%," Maya replied. "Below the compatibility threshold. Fundamentally incompatible. That's what the algorithm says."

"I don't care what the algorithm says."

"You should. We both should. Derek, we built this entire relationship on the premise that we were 97.8% compatible. That number gave us permission to try even though we seemed wrong for each other. And now—"

"And now we know that we tried anyway. We chose each other anyway. Maya, every date, every conversation, every moment—that was real. The algorithm might have been our excuse to start, but it wasn't why we continued."

"How do you know?" Maya's voice cracked. "How do you know we're not just fooling ourselves? What if we've been performing compatibility because we wanted the algorithm to be right?"

"Because I've been in a relationship where the algorithm was right. 95% compatible with Elena. Perfect on paper. And I was miserable." Derek stepped closer. "With you, I'm 71% compatible and happier than I've ever been. So you tell me—which number matters more?"

"But 71% means fundamental differences. It means we're going to struggle. It means—"

"It means we're going to have to work at this. It means it won't be easy." Derek was right in front of her now. "Maya, I don't want easy. I want real. And what we have is real."

"Is it?" Maya's eyes were swimming with tears. "Or did we just convince ourselves it was real because the algorithm told us to be together?"

"Do you love me?" Derek asked quietly.

"That's not fair—"

"Do you love me?" he repeated. "Because I love you. And I know that's real because it terrifies me. Because I stayed up all night after that email trying to figure out how to tell you, and every scenario ended with me losing you, and the thought of that made me physically ill. Because when you said 'I love you' last night, I felt it here—" He pressed his hand to his chest. "Not in my head where I analyze everything, but here. So do you love me?"

Maya was crying now, full tears streaming down her face. "Yes. God, yes, I love you. But Derek, what if love isn't enough? What if we're too different and we're just setting ourselves up to fail?"

"Then we fail." Derek cupped her face with both hands, thumbs wiping away tears. "But we fail together, having tried. Because the alternative—walking away right now because an algorithm says we might struggle—that's guaranteed failure. And I'm not ready to give up on us. Are you?"

Maya looked at him for a long moment, and Derek could see it—the war happening inside her. The urge to run, to protect herself, to choose adventure over risk. And the other pull—the one that made her stay, that made her want to try, that made her love him despite every instinct telling her to leave.

"I'm scared," she whispered.

"Me too."

"What if we can't make it work?"

"What if we can?"

"Derek—"

"Maya, I know I messed up. I should have told you about the email immediately. I should have trusted you to handle it. And I'm sorry—I'm so sorry I didn't." He pressed his forehead to hers. "But please don't let my mistake or the algorithm's correction be the reason we don't try. Let's fail on our own terms, not because some computer program said we would."

Maya's hands came up to grip his wrists, holding him there. "Promise me something."

"Anything."

"Promise me that if this gets too hard—if we're making each other miserable—we'll be honest about it. We won't stay together just to prove the algorithm wrong."

"I promise. But Maya, I also promise to fight for this. To work at this. To not let fundamental differences become deal-breakers." He pulled back slightly to look at her. "The algorithm says we're 71% compatible. Fine. Let's prove we can make that 71% enough."

"Or we could try to get to 72%," Maya said, and he heard the slight edge of humor breaking through.

"That's very ambitious of you."

"I'm an ambitious person." She was almost smiling now, even through tears. "Derek, I'm still mad at you for not telling me about the error immediately."

"That's fair."

"And I'm going to need time to process this. The number, what it means, how we move forward."

"I understand."

"But I'm not running. Not yet. Not—" She took a shaky breath. "Not if you're willing to actually work at this with me."

Derek kissed her then, soft and certain, tasting salt from her tears and hope from her words. When they pulled apart, he said, "I'm willing to work at this for as long as you'll let me."

"Good. Because I post-cried mascara is not a good look on me, and I've done it twice in one day for you. You better be worth it."

"I'll do my best."

They sat down on the amphitheater steps together, Maya leaning into his side, Derek's arm around her shoulders. The park was busy with Saturday afternoon activity—families, joggers, dogs playing—but it felt like they were in their own bubble.

"So what now?" Maya asked.

"Now we figure it out. Together. Without an algorithm telling us how."

"That's terrifying."

"Yeah." Derek kissed the top of her head. "But we've been pretty good at terrifying so far."

Maya's phone buzzed. She pulled it out—an Instagram notification. Someone had commented on her story.

> *@synapse_official: Sometimes the best matches are the ones that don't make sense on paper. We're rooting for you. - Dr. Torres*

Maya showed Derek. He read it, then looked at her with a slight smile.

"The algorithm is rooting for us even though it says we're incompatible. That's either very supportive or very contradictory."

"Maybe it's both." Maya screenshot the comment. "Should I post about this? The error, the 71%, all of it?"

"Do you want to?"

She thought about it. Her followers had been on this journey with her from the beginning. They'd watched her fall for Derek, watched them overcome obstacles, watched her grow.

"Yeah," she said. "I think I do. But not yet. First, I want to figure out what we are without the algorithm. Then I'll share it."

"What we are," Derek repeated. "I like the sound of that."

"Me too."

They sat there for a while longer, neither quite ready to move, both trying to figure out how to rebuild something that had just been shaken to its foundation.

Maya - Later That Evening

Maya posted at 9 PM, after she and Derek had spent the afternoon talking—really talking—about what the corrected score meant, what they wanted, what scared them.

The post was a photo of the Synapse app icon with a red "71.3%" overlaid on it. The caption:

Update on the #SynapseExperiment: Turns out there was an error. Our "97.8% compatibility" was actually 71.3%. According to the algorithm, that means we're fundamentally incompatible.

Here's what I know: Numbers on a screen can't tell you who to love. An algorithm can give you an introduction, but it can't build a relationship. That part is all you.

Derek and I are going to try to make 71% work. Not to prove the algorithm wrong, but because what we have feels right even when the data says it's wrong.

Maybe we'll fail spectacularly. Maybe in six months I'll be posting about why you should trust the algorithm. But maybe—just maybe—

we'll prove that compatibility is something you build, not something you're born with.

Love isn't math. And thank god for that.

#SynapseExperiment #71Percent #ChoosingUsAnyw

The post exploded immediately. Hundreds of comments within minutes:

@SuzieParksPhotography: Proud of you

@marcus_beats: My brother found a real one. Don't let her go bro

@wanderlust_adventures: THIS IS THE CONTENT I NEEDED

@elena_volkov: Rooting for you both

@synapse_official: Sometimes the best outcomes are the unexpected ones. Wishing you both the best on this journey. - The Synapse Team

And then, the one that made Maya's breath catch:

@derek_chen: 71% is just a starting point. Let's see how high we can get it. Together.

Maya screenshot that comment and sent it to him: *Did you just comment publicly on my Instagram post? Derek Chen, you're becoming a social media person*

Derek: *Don't get used to it*

Maya: *Too late. You're mine now. All 71% of you*

Derek: *All 100% of me. The algorithm doesn't get to decide how much of myself I give you*

Maya stared at that message, feeling something settle in her chest. They didn't have all the answers. They didn't know if 71% would be enough. But they were going to try.

And for Maya Reyes—chronic runner, perpetual wanderer, commitment-phobic traveler—choosing to try was the biggest adventure of all.

Derek

Derek sat in his apartment, reading through the comments on Maya's post, feeling something he hadn't felt in a long time: hope mixed with uncertainty, fear mixed with determination.

His phone rang. Dr. Michelle Torres, according to the caller ID. The founder of Synapse.

"Derek? This is Dr. Torres. I hope I'm not calling too late."

"No, it's fine. What can I do for you?"

"I wanted to reach out personally. Your match with Maya Reyes has been... exceptional to watch."

"You've been watching?"

"We monitor all matches for quality control and algorithm improvement. But yours has been particularly interesting." Dr. Torres paused. "Okay."

"The error was real. The 71.3% is accurate. But here's what the algorithm can't measure: growth. The compatibility score reflects who you were on the day you were matched. It doesn't account for who you become together. You and Maya have changed each other. You're more spontaneous. She's more grounded. Those changes aren't in the algorithm's calculations. If I ran your compatibility now, with who you've become over the past eight weeks, the score would be different."

"How different?"

"I don't know. That's the point. Human relationships are dynamic. The algorithm gives you a starting point, but it can't predict how you'll evolve together." She sighed.

"Why are you telling me this?"

"Because I saw Maya's Instagram post. Because I see how hard you're both trying. And because—" Dr. Torres laughed softly. "Because I'm rooting for you to prove that 71% is enough. It would be good data."

After they hung up, Derek opened his notes app and started writing: *Things the algorithm couldn't measure:*

- The way Maya makes me laugh at my own rigidity - How I've started leaving white space in my calendar - The fact that I'm not scared of spontaneity anymore - That she's learning to stay - That I'm learning to let go - That we choose each other every day - That love doesn't need 97.8% to be real.

He saved it, then sent it to Maya: *Things the algorithm got wrong about us*

Her response came immediately: *It got one thing right though*

Derek: *What's that?*

Maya: *That we were worth introducing.*

Derek smiled at his phone: *Best introduction I ever had. Even if the math was wrong.*

8. Building 71%

Three Weeks After The Revelation

WORKING AT IT

Week One: The Adjustment

Tuesday Evening - Maya's Place

Maya's house was chaos incarnate—Suzie's wedding photography equipment in one corner, Carlos's protein supplements covering the kitchen counter, Maya's travel gear exploding from her bedroom. Derek stood in the doorway, trying not to visibly wince at the disorder.

"I know it's messy," Maya said, watching his face. "You don't have to come here if it stresses you out. We can always hang out at your place."

"No." Derek stepped inside, deliberately setting down his bag in the middle of the floor instead of finding a designated spot. "I want to be comfortable in your space. I'm just... adjusting."

"You can adjust things if you need to. I won't be offended."

"Really?"

"Really. Just maybe don't alphabetize my spice rack like you did last time."

Derek had the grace to look embarrassed. "That was helpful organization."

"That was you having a panic attack about my kitchen." But Maya was smiling. "Come on. I'm attempting to cook dinner. It'll probably be a disaster."

She was making stir-fry—or attempting to. The kitchen was already a war zone of chopped vegetables, spilled soy sauce, and what appeared to be smoke from something burning.

"Maya, the garlic—"

"I know!" She grabbed the pan off the heat, waving away smoke. "See? This is why we're 71%. You would never burn garlic."

"I've burned garlic."

"When?"

"...Okay, never. But I could." Derek moved beside her, assessing the situation. "Can I help?"

"Can you take over without making me feel incompetent?"

"I'll try."

They cooked together—Derek salvaging the garlic situation, Maya chopping vegetables with her characteristic disregard for uniform sizes. It wasn't perfect. Derek had to consciously stop himself from correcting her technique three times. Maya had to consciously stop herself from getting defensive when he offered suggestions.

But they ate dinner on her couch, tangled together, watching a travel documentary Maya had picked, and it felt like progress.

"How are we doing?" Maya asked during a commercial break. "On the working-at-it scale."

"Better than I expected. Worse than I hoped." Derek kissed her temple. "But we're doing it."

"That's very diplomatic."

"I'm learning."

Thursday Afternoon - Derek's Office

Derek was in the middle of a financial model when his phone rang. Maya, FaceTime.

He almost declined—he was at work, he had a meeting in twenty minutes, this was his professional space—but he'd promised to be more spontaneous. More available.

He answered.

Maya's face filled the screen, and she was at the airport. Of course she was.

"Don't panic," she said immediately.

"I'm panicking."

"It's just a quick trip. Three days. A brand wants me to do content in Portland, and it's good money, and I have to take it." She was walking through the terminal, camera bouncing. "I know we were supposed to have dinner tomorrow, and I'm sorry, but—"

"It's fine," Derek interrupted, forcing his voice to stay level. "It's your job. I understand."

"Are you sure? Because you have your 'I'm saying it's fine but it's not fine' voice."

Derek took a breath. This was the work—being honest about what he felt instead of pretending everything was okay. "I'm disappointed. I was looking forward to tomorrow. But I also understand that this is your career, and you need to take opportunities when they come."

"There he is." Maya's smile was soft. "Honest Derek. I like him."

"Can you text me when you land?"

"I can do better than that. I'll send you photos. Annoying amounts of photos. You'll get sick of my face."

"Impossible."

"Challenge accepted."

She did text when she landed. And sent photos—too many photos, of her hotel room, of Portland bridges, of food carts, of a busker playing guitar on the street. Derek found himself smiling at his phone during meetings, which was unprofessional and unlike him and somehow perfect.

Derek: *You're right. I am getting sick of your face*

Maya: *LIES. You love my face*

Derek: *I really do*

Maya: *Miss you already*

Derek: *You've been gone four hours*

Maya: *Your point?*

Three days felt longer than it should have. But Maya came back on Sunday evening, jet-lagged and carrying coffee she'd bought him at the Portland airport, and Derek realized something: she'd left, but she'd come back. She always came back.

That was growth.

Week Two: The Fight

Saturday Morning - Hiking Disagreement

It started small, the way these things always did.

They were supposed to go hiking at Rancho San Antonio—Derek's plan, carefully mapped out, with a specific trail and timeline. But when he picked Maya up, she had a different idea.

"What if we tried Purisima Creek instead? I saw photos online, and it looks amazing."

"That's forty-five minutes away. We'd have to completely restructure the timing."

"So? We'll restructure." Maya was already pulling up directions on her phone. "Come on, be spontaneous."

"I am spontaneous. But Purisima is a harder trail, we're not prepared for the elevation gain, and we'd get back after dark."

"We have flashlights on our phones."

"Maya, I planned Rancho San Antonio. I researched the trail, I calculated the timing—"

"You calculated hiking?" Maya's voice had an edge to it. "Derek, it's a walk in the woods, not a military operation."

"I like being prepared. That's not a character flaw."

"I didn't say it was. I just think maybe you could be a little more flexible sometimes."

"And I think maybe you could commit to a plan once in a while instead of constantly trying to change everything at the last minute."

The car went silent. Maya stared out the window, jaw tight. Derek gripped the steering wheel, already regretting his tone.

"Should we just go home?" Maya asked quietly.

"No. Let's—" Derek took a breath. "Let's go to Purisima Creek."

"I don't want you to go if you're going to be miserable about it."

"I won't be miserable. I'm just... adjusting my expectations. Which is part of the work, right?"

Maya looked at him, searching his face. "Are you sure?"

"No. But I'm willing to try."

They went to Purisima Creek. It was beautiful—redwoods and creek crossings and views Derek would never have seen if they'd stuck to his plan. It was also harder than he'd expected, they did get back after dark, and he was exhausted in a way his carefully planned hikes never left him.

But Maya's face when they reached the overlook—the pure joy in it—made it worth it.

"Thank you," she said, squeezing his hand. "For being flexible."

"Thank you for pushing me." Derek pulled her close. "Even when I'm being rigid."

"You're not rigid. You're structured. There's a difference."

"Is there?"

"Yeah. Rigid means you can't bend. Structured means you have a framework but you can adapt within it." She kissed him. "You're adapting. I see it."

"So are you. You committed to a plan for the first twenty minutes before trying to change it. That's progress."

"We're a work in progress."

"71% work in progress."

"Climbing to 72," Maya said with determination.

Friday Night - The Calendar Compromise

Derek had started keeping two calendars: his original color-coded system, and a shared digital calendar with Maya that was significantly less organized.

On Friday, he opened the shared calendar to add their dinner plans and found Maya had already added something: "Spontaneous Adventure - TBD."

He called her immediately.

"Did you schedule spontaneity?" he asked, trying not to sound amused.

"I'm learning your language. If I put it on the calendar, you won't panic when I suggest something unplanned."

"That's... actually really thoughtful."

"I know. I'm adapting." He could hear her smile. "You're rubbing off on me. Last week I meal-prepped. Just one meal, but still. Suzie almost fainted."

"And you're rubbing off on me. I left Saturday completely unscheduled."

"Completely?"

"Completely. Just blank space. For whatever happens."

"Derek Chen, I'm so proud of you I could cry."

"Please don't cry."

"Too late. I'm getting emotional about your calendar growth."

They met for their scheduled/unscheduled Friday dinner, and Maya pulled out a small notebook.

"What's that?" Derek asked.

"I'm trying something. A compromise." She opened it to show him. "I'm terrible at planning ahead, right? But you need plans to feel secure. So I'm keeping a list of things I want to do—places I want to go, restaurants I want to try, adventures I want to have. That way, when you ask what I want to do, I have options instead of just saying 'I don't know, something fun.'"

Derek took the notebook, reading through her list. It was very Maya—half specific ("Try the new ramen place on Castro"), half vague ("Go somewhere we've never been"), all enthusiastic.

"This is really good," he said.

"Yeah?"

"Yeah. Can I add to it?"

"You want to add to my spontaneity list?"

"I want to contribute to our adventure list." Derek pulled out a pen, started writing. "Some of these need structure to make happen. Like this one—'Weekend trip somewhere new.' We should pick a date, book accommodations—"

"You're organizationally supporting my chaos."

"I'm providing framework for your spontaneity." He looked up at her. "Is that okay?"

"It's perfect." Maya leaned across the table to kiss him. "This is what 71% building to 72% looks like."

Week Three: The Integration

Tuesday Evening - Meeting Friends

"My friends want to meet you," Maya said, scrolling through texts. "There's a group dinner Wednesday at this new Korean place in Sunnyvale. Very casual, very loud, probably chaotic."

Derek felt his anxiety spike. He'd met Suzie multiple times now, but Suzie was one person. A group of Maya's friends—creative, spontaneous, probably used to her dating equally spontaneous people—felt overwhelming.

"How many people?" he asked.

"Maybe eight? Ten? Some people might bring plus-ones." Maya looked at him carefully. "If it's too much—"

"No. I want to meet your friends. I just... need to prepare."

"How do you prepare for meeting friends?"

"I don't know. Research? What do they do? What do they like? What should I talk about?"

Maya set down her phone, took both his hands. "Derek, they're going to love you. Or they're going to be confused by you. Possibly both. But they care about me, and you make me happy, so they'll care about you."

"What if I'm too boring? What if they think—"

"Stop." She squeezed his hands. "You're not boring. We've established this. You're structured and thoughtful and you do this thing where you actually listen when people talk instead of just waiting for your turn. My friends are going to appreciate that."

Wednesday night, Derek showed up to the Korean restaurant in jeans and a button-down—casual for him, probably overdressed for the setting. Maya was already there, surrounded by people who were exactly as she'd described: loud, animated, warm.

"Everyone, this is Derek!" Maya pulled him into the group. "Derek, this is everyone. I'll do individual names later when it's quieter."

It was overwhelming. The restaurant was packed, the conversation overlapping, people ordering food family-style without consulting him about preferences. Derek found himself sitting between Maya and a guy named Kevin who worked in film production and wanted to talk about the economics of streaming services.

"So you're the algorithm guy," Kevin said, halfway through dinner. "Maya's been posting about you."

"I'm Derek. The algorithm was just the introduction."

"Right, but you stuck it out even after the score dropped. That's commitment." Kevin gestured with his chopsticks. "Most people would've bailed. Easier to blame the algorithm than do the work."

"Bailing wasn't an option."

"Why not?"

Derek looked at Maya, who was deep in conversation with two other friends, laughing at something, her whole face lit up. "Because she's worth the work."

"Good answer." Kevin nodded approvingly. "Okay, you're passing the friend test."

"There's a test?"

"There's always a test." But Kevin was smiling. "You're doing fine. Just don't hurt her, and we're good."

By the end of the night, Derek had learned everyone's names, contributed to three different conversations, and even laughed at his own expense when Maya told the story of him alphabetizing her spice rack.

"You alphabetized her spices?" one friend asked, incredulous.

"They were in complete disarray," Derek said defensively.

"They were FINE," Maya protested.

"They were chaos."

"You love chaos."

"I love your chaos." Derek pulled her close. "There's a difference."

In the car afterward, Maya was beaming. "You survived. You more than survived—Kevin likes you, and Kevin doesn't like anyone."

"He seems nice."

"He is, but he's protective. The fact that he gave you his approval means a lot." She squeezed his hand. "Thank you for doing that. I know big groups aren't your thing."

"They're not. But you're my thing. So I'm learning to adapt."

Saturday Afternoon - Teaching Derek to be Spontaneous

Maya had declared Saturday "Spontaneity Training Day." Derek had immediately tried to make an itinerary.

"No," she'd said, taking away his notebook. "That defeats the purpose. Today, we're doing whatever feels right in the moment."

"But how do I prepare if I don't know what we're doing?"

"You don't prepare. That's the point."

They started at the farmers market, where Maya made Derek close his eyes and pick a random vegetable. He got kohlrabi, which neither of them had ever cooked.

"What do we do with this?" Derek asked, examining it.

"We figure it out. That's the adventure."

From there, they wandered—no destination, no timeline. They found a used bookstore and spent an hour browsing. Maya bought three books she'd never heard of, chosen purely by cover. Derek bought one book he'd been meaning to read for months and felt slightly guilty about the practicality of his choice.

"You're allowed to be practical," Maya assured him. "This isn't about becoming a different person. It's about stretching."

They ended up at a small art gallery having a free exhibition opening. Derek would never have gone on his own—art galleries made him feel inadequate, like he should understand things he didn't. But Maya walked through with enthusiasm, creating stories about the paintings, making him laugh.

"What do you see?" she asked, pointing to an abstract piece—all blues and grays and chaotic brushstrokes.

"Honestly? Expensive chaos."

"Look closer. What feeling does it give you?"

Derek studied it, trying to see past his discomfort with not understanding. "Uncertainty," he said finally. "But also... movement. Like even though everything's unclear, there's forward motion."

"Exactly." Maya smiled. "That's us. Moving forward even when we can't see the full picture."

"That's very metaphorical."

"I contain multitudes."

They cooked the kohlrabi that night—looked up recipes on their phones, improvised with what they had, ended up with something surprisingly edible. They ate it on Derek's couch, Maya's feet in his lap, talking about nothing important.

"How do you feel?" Maya asked. "After a whole day of no planning?"

"Exhausted," Derek admitted. "But good. Like I exercised a muscle I usually don't use."

"That's exactly what it is. You're building spontaneity muscles."

"And you're building planning muscles."

"We're becoming hybrids. Planners who can be spontaneous. Spontaneous people who can commit to plans."

"71% originals," Derek said. "Working toward our own version of 100%."

Sunday Evening - The Check-In

They'd instituted Sunday evening check-ins—Maya's therapist's suggestion, which she'd shared with Derek. A dedicated time to talk about how they were feeling, what was working, what wasn't.

"Okay," Maya said, sitting cross-legged on Derek's couch with her notebook. "Highs and lows of the week."

"High: Meeting your friends went better than I feared," Derek said. "Low: I still had a minor panic attack about the unstructured day yesterday."

"You hid it well."

"Practice." He squeezed her hand. "Your turn."

"High: You were amazing with my friends. Like, genuinely amazing. Low: I almost booked a flight to Mexico on Wednesday when work was stressful, but I stopped myself because we had plans."

"You stopped yourself from running?"

"I'm trying. It's hard." Maya's voice was small. "My instinct is still to leave when things feel heavy. But I'm learning to sit with the discomfort instead."

"That's huge progress."

"It doesn't feel huge. It feels like I'm fighting my own brain constantly."

"That's what growth is." Derek pulled her closer. "Fighting your instincts until new instincts develop."

"How are you really doing?" Maya asked. "With the 71%? Be honest."

Derek thought about it. "Some days I forget about it entirely. We're just us, and the number doesn't matter. Other days, I worry that we're forcing something that isn't meant to work. That we're trying so hard to prove the algorithm wrong that we're not seeing reality."

"What's reality?"

"Reality is that I love you. Reality is that you make me want to be more flexible, and I seem to make you want to be more grounded. Reality is that we're different in fundamental ways, and sometimes that's hard, but it's also what makes this interesting."

"So we're working?"

"We're working. Not perfectly, but—"

"But working." Maya kissed him softly. "That's enough. For now, that's enough."

***

9. Present Day: Three Weeks After The Revelation

Maya

Maya was editing photos from their spontaneous Saturday when her phone rang. Unknown number.

"Hello?"

"Hi, Maya? This is Dr. Michelle Torres from Synapse. Do you have a few minutes?"

Maya sat up straighter. "Dr. Torres. Hi. Yes, I have time."

"I wanted to check in on you and Derek. I saw your Instagram posts—you've been very open about the journey. How are things going?"

"They're... good? Hard, but good. We're working at it."

"That's exactly what I hoped to hear." Dr. Torres sounded genuinely pleased. "Maya, can I share something with you? Something I haven't shared publicly?"

"Okay."

"The algorithm is very good at predicting initial compatibility—the ease of starting a relationship. But it's terrible at predicting long-term success. You know why?"

"Why?"

"Because long-term success isn't about starting compatibility. It's about commitment, communication, and willingness to grow. Those aren't things the algorithm can measure." She paused. "Your 71.3% means you started from different places. But the work you're both doing? That's building something the algorithm could never predict."

"So you're saying we might actually make it?"

"I'm saying you're doing everything right. The couples who make it aren't the ones with the highest scores. They're the ones who choose each other every day, even when it's hard. You and Derek are doing that."

After the call, Maya sat with that information for a while. Then she opened Instagram and posted:

Week 3 update on trying to make 71% work:

We fought about hiking trails. We compromised on calendars. He met my chaotic friends. I'm learning to make plans. He's learning to break them.

It's not always pretty. But it's real.

The algorithm gave us a number. We're giving it meaning.

#SynapseExperiment #71Percent #BuildingCompatibility

The comments came quickly:

> *@SuzieParksPhotography: So proud of you both*
>
> *@derek_chen: Building something better than the algorithm predicted*
>
> *@synapse_official: This is exactly what we hoped to see. Growth beyond the numbers. Keep going.*
>
> *@elena_volkov: You two are doing the hard work. It shows.*

And then, one comment that made Maya's heart stop:

@james_park: Derek, check your email. Something's come up with Synapse. Call me.

Maya screenshot it immediately, sent it to Derek: *What does James mean?*

Three dots appeared, then disappeared. Then appeared again.

Finally: *I don't know. Let me call him*

Derek

Derek called James immediately, stepping out of his home office.

"What's going on?"

"Check your email," James said. "Like, right now. From Synapse."

Derek opened his laptop with a sinking feeling. There was an email from Dr. Torres, marked urgent:

Subject: Compatibility Re-Assessment - Match #2847 - URGENT

Dear Derek and Maya,

We need to speak with you both urgently regarding your match.

We've discovered an additional error in our audit process. The 71.3% compatibility score we provided three weeks ago was based on a flawed re-calculation methodology.

We've completed a full system review with external auditors, and we need to share the findings with you both immediately.

Can you come to our Palo Alto office tomorrow (Monday) at 10:00 AM? Both of you need to be present.

This is time-sensitive and important.

I apologize for the continued uncertainty.

Dr. Michelle Torres
Founder & CEO, Synapse AI

Derek read it twice, his heart racing.

"Another error?" he said to James. "There was another error in the re-calculation?"

"That's what Elena's email says too. We're supposed to go in tomorrow as well. Whatever this is, it affects multiple matches from that time-frame."

"What do you think it means?"

"I have no idea, man. But Derek—" James paused. "Whatever the number is this time, you and Maya are solid. I've seen you two together. Don't let another algorithm correction mess that up."

After hanging up, Derek immediately called Maya.

"Another error," he said when she answered.

"I saw. James posted that comment before the email came through."

"They want us in Palo Alto tomorrow at 10 AM. Both of us."

"Derek, I—" Maya's voice was shaky. "I can't do this again. I can't get another number that tells us we're wrong for each other. We've worked so hard these past three weeks—"

"I know."

"What if it's even lower? What if it's like 50% or 30% or—"

"Maya, stop." Derek took a breath. "Whatever the number is tomorrow, it doesn't change what we've built. It doesn't change that I love you or that we've been making this work."

"But what if—"

"No what-ifs. We go tomorrow, we hear what they have to say, and then we decide—together—what it means for us. Not what it means for the algorithm. For us."

Maya was quiet for a long moment. "Okay," she said finally. "Okay. Together."

"Together. Always."

"Derek?"

"Yeah?"

"I'm scared."

"Me too. But we've been scared before. We'll handle this one too."

After they hung up, Derek sat in his home office, staring at the email, trying to prepare for every possibility. The financial analyst in him wanted to run scenarios, calculate probabilities, create contingency plans.

But the man who'd spent three weeks learning to be spontaneous made himself close the laptop.

Whatever happened tomorrow, they'd face it together.

No amount of preparation could change that.

He leaned back in his chair, listening to the unfamiliar silence of a room that used to be his entire world. For years, his worth had been measured in spreadsheets and the predictability of a well-executed hedge. But as he watched the cursor blink on the dark screen, he realized the last twenty-one days had rewritten his internal code. The safety wasn't in the data anymore; it was in the memory of her laughter and the way they'd navigated the unknown without a map. He didn't need a projected outcome to feel steady.

***

10. The Truth About Compatibility

Monday, 9:45 AM - Synapse AI Headquarters, Palo Alto

Maya

Maya had changed outfits three times that morning before settling on jeans and a blazer—professional enough for a tech company meeting, comfortable enough that she wouldn't fidget constantly. Derek had picked her up at 9:15, both of them quiet during the drive, holding hands across the center console like they were heading into battle.

Which, in a way, they were.

Synapse AI's headquarters was in a sleek modern building on University Avenue, all glass and steel and the kind of minimalist design that screamed "we have venture capital money." The lobby had a wall-sized screen displaying real-time match statistics: "47,293 active matches. 94.2% satisfaction rate. 23,847 successful long-term relationships."

"They really believe in their algorithm," Derek murmured.

"They built a company on it," Maya replied. "Of course they believe in it."

A receptionist led them to a conference room on the third floor. James and Elena were already there, sitting on one side of a long table, both looking equally nervous. Elena gave

Maya a small, supportive smile. James clapped Derek on the shoulder.

"Whatever this is," James said quietly, "we're all in it together."

Before anyone could respond, Dr. Michelle Torres entered, followed by two other people—a young woman with purple hair carrying a laptop, and an older man in a suit who radiated "legal counsel."

"Thank you all for coming on short notice," Dr. Torres said, taking a seat at the head of the table. "I know this has been a stressful journey for both couples. I want to start by apologizing—again—for the errors in our system. What should have been a straightforward matching process has become something much more complicated."

"What's the number this time?" Maya asked, unable to help herself. "Just tell us. Are we 50%? 40%? Should we just break up now and save everyone the trouble?"

"Maya—" Derek started.

"No, it's a fair question," Dr. Torres said. She looked at the young woman with purple hair, who opened her laptop. "Kira here is our lead algorithm architect. Kira, can you explain what we found?"

Kira cleared her throat, clearly uncomfortable being the center of attention. "So, okay. When we did the audit three weeks ago after discovering the initial error, we ran your compatibility scores through our standard re-calculation protocol. That's how we got the 71.3% for Maya and Derek, and the corrected scores for the other matches affected by the server timeout."

"But?" Derek prompted.

"But we made an assumption in that re-calculation that turned out to be wrong." Kira pulled up a screen showing complex graphs and data points. "Our algorithm has two modes: predictive compatibility—which measures how compatible people are at the moment of matching—and adaptive compatibility, which accounts for how people might change in a relationship. We ran your re-calculations using only predictive compatibility."

"What does that mean?" Elena asked.

"It means," Dr. Torres said, taking over, "that the 71.3% score was accurate for who Derek and Maya were on March 15th when they were first matched. But it didn't account for who they might become together."

Maya's heart was pounding. "I don't understand."

"Our algorithm is designed to be dynamic," Kira continued. "It's supposed to track how matches evolve over time, measuring changes in behavior, communication patterns, shared experiences, and personal growth. For most matches, this happens automatically in the background. But for the matches affected by the server timeout, that adaptive tracking was disabled."

She pulled up another screen—this one showing two lines on a graph. One was labeled "Initial Compatibility: 97.8%" and stayed flat. The other started at "Corrected Compatibility: 71.3%" and then began to climb, week by week.

"We manually ran the adaptive algorithm on your match," Kira said. "Taking into account every date, every interaction we could track through the app, your social media posts, and the growth patterns we observed. The algorithm measured how you've changed each other, how you've compromised, how you've built compatibility through effort."

Maya stared at the climbing line, barely breathing.

"Your current compatibility score," Dr. Torres said, "as of this morning, accounting for three weeks of active relationship work, is 89.7%."

The room went silent.

"What?" Maya whispered.

"89.7%," Dr. Torres repeated. "You started at 71.3%. In three weeks, through conscious effort and genuine growth, you've built yourselves to 89.7%. That's extraordinary."

Derek was staring at the screen, looking like he'd been hit with something heavy. "That's not possible. We're still fighting about basic things. We're still learning how to compromise. How can we be 89.7%?"

"Because compatibility isn't about never fighting," the man in the suit said—Maya realized this must be someone from legal or perhaps a relationship expert Synapse kept on staff. "It's about having the skills to resolve conflicts. It's about choosing to grow toward each other. The algorithm measures that now."

"Wait," James said, leaning forward. "What about us? Elena and I?"

Kira pulled up another graph. "Your initial match was calculated correctly at 94.1%. With three weeks of adaptive tracking, you're now at 96.3%. You started high and you're growing steadily. That's the more traditional pattern we see."

Elena reached for James's hand under the table. "So we're good?"

"You're very good," Dr. Torres confirmed. "But here's what's interesting—" She gestured at both graphs side by side. "Maya and Derek's rate of compatibility growth is unprecedented. Most couples who start at 71% either stay there or decline. You two have climbed eighteen percentage points in three weeks. That suggests something powerful about how well you work together."

Maya couldn't process this. Three weeks ago, she'd been ready to walk away because they were "fundamentally incompatible." Now the same algorithm was saying they were approaching the threshold of "exceptional long-term compatibility."

"I don't understand how we did this," Maya said, looking at Derek. "We're still so different."

"You are different," Dr. Torres agreed. "But you're different in complementary ways now. Derek, you've become 23% more spontaneous in your decision-making patterns, based on your digital footprint. Maya, you've become 31% more structured in your planning behaviors. You're not becoming identical—you're meeting in the middle."

"The algorithm can measure that?" Derek asked, sounding slightly unsettled.

"With permission, yes. All app users consent to behavioral tracking for algorithm improvement." Kira pulled up more data. "We track communication frequency, response times, emotional content of messages, shared activities, social media posts, calendar patterns. We build a comprehensive picture of relationship health."

"That's incredibly invasive," Maya said.

"It's what you signed up for," the legal counsel said smoothly. "But you can opt out of tracking at any time. Many couples do, after they're confident in their match."

"What happens if we opt out?" Derek asked. "Do we stop getting scores?"

"You stop getting updates, yes. But more importantly—" Dr. Torres leaned forward, "—you stop needing them. The algorithm's purpose is to help people find compatible matches and support them through early relationship development. Once you're established, you don't need us anymore."

Maya looked at the graph again, at that climbing line showing how hard they'd worked, how far they'd come. 89.7%. Eighteen points in three weeks.

"If we'd known the score was climbing," Maya said slowly, "would we have worked as hard?"

The question hung in the air.

"That's actually why we didn't tell you," Dr. Torres admitted. "We wanted to see if you'd continue growing without the validation of increasing numbers. We wanted to see if your commitment to each other was about the relationship or about proving the algorithm right."

"That's manipulative," Derek said, voice hard.

"It is," Dr. Torres agreed. "And I apologize. But Derek, Maya—the fact that you kept working, kept choosing each other, even when you thought you were fundamentally incompatible? That tells us more about your relationship than any score ever could."

"So this was a test," Maya said. "The 71.3% was real, but you were testing whether we'd quit or keep going."

"Not exactly. The 71.3% was accurate for who you were then. We didn't manipulate that. But we did choose not to share the adaptive tracking because..." Dr. Torres smiled slightly. "Because you two were the most interesting match we'd ever seen. Two people who seemed completely wrong for each other, working harder than any couple with a 95%+ score. We wanted to study it."

"We were your experiment," Derek said flatly.

"You were participants in a study, yes. All matches are, technically—that's in the terms of service. But you were a particularly fascinating case study in whether compatibility can be built rather than just discovered."

Maya felt something shift in her chest—anger, maybe, or betrayal. "You let us think we were failing when we were actually succeeding?"

"You were never failing. The work you were doing was exactly what successful couples do. We just wanted to see if you'd do it without external validation." Dr. Torres's expression was genuinely apologetic. "I know this feels like a betrayal. But Maya, Derek—look at what you built. You did that without knowing the algorithm was on your side. That makes it real."

Maya looked at Derek, trying to gauge his reaction. His face was carefully neutral—the expression he used when he was processing something big.

"Can we have a minute?" Derek asked. "Just the two of us?"

"Of course." Dr. Torres stood, gesturing to the others. "We'll step out. Take your time."

The room emptied, leaving Maya and Derek alone with the graph still displayed on the screen, that climbing line mocking them with its upward trajectory.

"So," Maya said. "89.7%."

"89.7%," Derek repeated. "Built from 71.3% in three weeks."

"Are you mad? I'm mad. I think I'm mad."

"I'm..." Derek stood up, paced to the window. "I don't know what I am. Part of me is angry that they watched us struggle without telling us it was working. Part of me is relieved that the work we did mattered. Part of me is..."

"Wondering if any of this is real?" Maya finished. "Because that's where I am. Derek, we made decisions based on thinking we were 71% compatible. We fought. We compromised. We changed. But if we'd known we were climbing, would we have done it differently?"

"I don't think so." Derek turned to face her. "Maya, I didn't work on us because I thought the score would go up. I worked on us because I couldn't imagine not working on us. The number didn't matter."

"Didn't it though? We met because of a number. We trusted each other because of a number. We almost broke up because of a number. Numbers have always mattered in this relationship."

"Maybe in the beginning. But somewhere along the way—" Derek crossed back to her, took both her hands.

"Somewhere along the way, I stopped caring about what the algorithm said. I just cared about you."

Maya felt tears pricking her eyes. "When? When did you stop caring?"

"The day you met my friends," Derek said immediately. "No—actually, before that. The farmers market. When I was watching you pick out vegetables and I realized I wanted to do that every week for the rest of my life. The algorithm didn't tell me that. I just... knew."

"For me it was the spontaneity day," Maya admitted. "When you were uncomfortable in the art gallery but stayed anyway because I wanted to be there. When you tried to see the painting the way I saw it instead of just saying you didn't get it. That's when I knew this wasn't about the algorithm anymore."

"So what do we do now?" Derek asked. "We're 89.7%. That's high. That's 'strong compatibility with manageable differences.' That's almost 'exceptional long-term compatibility.'"

"Do we keep tracking? Do we try to get to 95%?"

"Do we want to?" Derek pulled her closer. "Maya, I don't want to spend our relationship chasing a number. I want to spend it being together. Making mistakes. Fighting about hiking trails. Compromising on calendars. Building something that's ours, not the algorithm's."

Maya looked at the screen one more time, at that climbing line showing their growth. Then she looked at Derek—at the man who'd learned to be spontaneous for her, who'd met her chaotic friends, who'd worked harder than anyone to make an incompatible match into something beautiful.

"Let's opt out," she said. "Let's turn off the tracking and just be us. No more scores, no more updates. Just us figuring it out."

"Are you sure?"

"I'm sure that I love you more than I love being right. And I'm sure that no algorithm can measure that." She smiled. "Besides, we already proved we can build compatibility from 71% to 89%. Imagine what we can do without anyone watching."

Derek kissed her then—soft and certain and full of everything words couldn't capture. When they pulled apart, he kept his forehead pressed to hers.

"Should we tell them?"

"Let's tell them together."

They walked to the door, opened it to find Dr. Torres, Kira, and the legal counsel waiting in the hallway. James and Elena were there too, standing close together, clearly having had their own processing conversation.

"We want to opt out of tracking," Maya said. "Both of us. No more scores, no more updates."

Dr. Torres smiled—genuinely smiled, like she'd been hoping for this. "That's exactly what I was hoping you'd say."

"Really?" Derek asked, suspicious.

"Really. The couples who opt out are the ones who've internalized the growth. They don't need external validation anymore. They know what they have." She pulled out a tablet. "I just need both of you to confirm the decision."

They did, signatures on a digital form that felt both momentous and simple.

"What about us?" James asked. "Should we opt out too?"

"That's entirely up to you," Dr. Torres said. "Elena?"

Elena looked at James, had some kind of silent conversation, then nodded. "We'll stay in. We started high, and I want to see how high we can go. Is that weird?"

"Not at all. Different couples need different things." Dr. Torres smiled at all four of them. "I have to say, this has been the most educational matching cohort we've ever studied. James and Elena—you proved that high initial compatibility can grow even higher with effort. Maya and Derek—you proved that low initial compatibility isn't destiny, that the right people can build something extraordinary from an unpromising start."

"So we're your success stories," Maya said drily. "Your data points."

"You're proof that the algorithm works, but not in the way people think." Dr. Torres gestured to the conference room. "Can we talk for a few more minutes? I have something I'd like to share with all of you."

Back in the conference room, Dr. Torres pulled up a presentation on the screen.

"I founded Synapse five years ago after my own marriage failed. We were perfect on paper—same background, same education, same goals. And we were miserable. I became obsessed with the question: why do some couples work and others don't?" She advanced to a slide showing early algorithm designs. "I built Synapse to answer that question. To create the perfect matching system."

"But?" Derek prompted.

"But I learned something over five years and 47,000 matches. There is no perfect matching system. Because compatibility isn't static—it's dynamic. It's not about finding someone identical to you; it's about finding someone who makes you want to grow. Someone who challenges you to be better while accepting who you are."

She pulled up the graph of Maya and Derek's growth again. "Your match was a mistake—twice. First, we calculated it too high. Then we calculated it without accounting for growth. But the mistake led to the discovery. It showed us that our algorithm was measuring the wrong thing."

"What should it be measuring?" Elena asked.

"Not compatibility at the start. Potential for growth. Not how well you match on day one, but how well you could match if you both chose to work at it." Dr. Torres looked directly at Maya and Derek. "Your 71.3% wasn't a failure. It was a starting point. And the fact that you chose to work from that starting point, without knowing it would pay off—that's what real love looks like."

Maya felt Derek's hand find hers under the table.

"So what happens now?" James asked. "You change the algorithm?"

"We're already changing it. Because of what we learned from your cohort, we're implementing adaptive scoring for all matches. Not just showing people their initial compatibility, but showing them their potential." She smiled. "You four are literally changing how people date."

"We're pioneers," Maya deadpanned. "How exciting."

"It is exciting," Dr. Torres said seriously. "You're proving that love is a choice, not just a calculation. That you can build compatibility through effort and commitment. That's revolutionary in a world that wants everything to be easy and instant."

They wrapped up the meeting with administrative details—refunds processed, data anonymized for research papers, permission for case studies. As they all stood to leave, Dr. Torres pulled Maya and Derek aside.

"Can I give you both some advice? Off the record?"

"Sure," Derek said.

"Stop posting about the experiment. Stop making your relationship content for Instagram. Make it just yours." She smiled. "You don't owe anyone an explanation or an ending to this story. The only people who need to know how this turns out are you two."

Maya thought about her Instagram, about the thousands of people who'd been following their journey, waiting for the resolution. About the engagement metrics, the comments, the investment.

"That's probably good advice," she admitted.

Outside, in the parking lot, the four of them stood by their cars for a moment, processing everything.

"So," James said. "That was intense."

"That's an understatement," Elena replied. She looked at Maya and Derek. "Are you two okay?"

"I think so?" Maya looked at Derek for confirmation.

"We're good," Derek said firmly. "Better than good. We're 89.7% and climbing."

"Not tracking, remember?" Maya nudged him.

"Right. We're undefined percentage and climbing."

James laughed. "Man, three months ago, you were color-coding your calendar and Elena was my best friend's ex-fiancée. Now look at us."

"The algorithm works in mysterious ways," Elena said, but she was smiling.

"Or it doesn't work at all, and we're just people making choices," Maya countered. "Either way, I'm glad we met. All of us."

"Even though it was messy and complicated and involved multiple compatibility scores?" Elena asked.

"Especially because of that." Maya squeezed Derek's hand. "The messy, complicated things are the real things."

They said their goodbyes—hugs, promises to get dinner soon without Synapse scheduling it. Then Maya and Derek got in his car, and he started the engine but didn't put it in gear.

"You okay?" Maya asked.

"89.7%," Derek said, staring at the steering wheel. "We built compatibility. From scratch. Through work."

"We did."

"That's insane."

"That's love." Maya turned to face him. "Derek, do you regret opting out of tracking? Do you wish we could see the number keep climbing?"

"No." He looked at her, certain. "I don't need to see a number to know what we have is real. Do you?"

"No. I trust us more than I trust the algorithm." She paused. "That's growth, right? Three months ago, I trusted the algorithm completely. Now I trust us more."

"That's definitely growth." Derek finally put the car in gear. "Where to? Lunch? Back to work? Your place?"

"Surprise me," Maya said.

Derek smiled—the full, genuine smile that he used to reserve for perfect outcomes but now used for her. "Okay. I will."

He drove, and Maya didn't ask where they were going, and for the first time in her life, the not-knowing felt like freedom instead of fear.

Maya - That Evening

Maya sat on her bed, staring at her Instagram app, her last post still up from that morning:

Heading to Synapse for another reveal. Whatever the number is, we're us. That's what matters. #SynapseExperiment #71Percent #ChoosingLove

The comments were already full of people asking for updates:

What happened??
TELL US THE SCORE
Are you guys still together???
We need an update!!!

Maya opened a new post, selected a photo from earlier—one Derek had taken of her at the farmers market weeks ago, mid-laugh, completely herself. She typed:

Final update on the #SynapseExperiment:

The algorithm was wrong. Then it was right. Then it was wrong again. Then it was more right than we expected.

Here's what matters: Derek and I chose each other at 97.8%. We chose each other at 71.3%. We chose each other at 89.7%.

And now we're choosing each other at undefined%, with no algorithm watching, no scores updating, no data tracking our growth.

We're just two people who met because of math and stayed because of choice.

Thank you for following this journey. But from here, it's ours.

No more numbers. Just us.

She posted it before she could overthink, then immediately turned off Instagram notifications.

Suzie knocked on her door. "You okay?"

"Yeah." Maya set down her phone. "I just ended the experiment. Publicly."

"How does it feel?"

"Scary. Liberating. Right." Maya smiled. "I built a whole platform on sharing everything, and now I'm choosing to keep the best thing private."

"That's massive growth, May."

"I know. Derek's influence." She lay back on her bed. "Suzie, I think I'm staying. Like, really staying. Not just 'staying until I get scared' but actually building a life here. With him."

"I'm so proud of you." Suzie sat beside her. "Three months ago, you couldn't commit to dinner plans."

"Three months ago, I didn't know what I was running from." Maya looked at her ceiling. "Turns out I was running from the possibility that staying could be better than leaving. That roots could feel like freedom instead of a trap."

"And now?"

"Now I'm learning that adventure doesn't have to be somewhere else. It can be right here, building something real with someone who sees me."

Her phone buzzed. Derek: *Saw your post. Thank you for choosing us over content*

Maya: *Thank you for being worth choosing*

Derek: *Tomorrow night. I'm planning something. Be ready by 7*

Maya: *Planning what?*

Derek: *If I told you, it wouldn't be spontaneous*

Maya: *Derek Chen is planning a surprise. I'm so proud*

Derek: *You're corrupting me*

Maya: *You're welcome*

She put her phone down and smiled at her ceiling, feeling something settle in her chest that she'd never felt before: certainty. Not about what would happen tomorrow or next month or next year. But certainty that whatever happened, they'd figure it out together.

That was enough.

More than enough.

That was everything.

***

Epilogue: Six Months Later

Six Months After Opting Out

Maya - October, Saturday Morning

Maya woke up to sunlight filtering through unfamiliar curtains and the smell of coffee brewing. For a disorienting moment, she couldn't remember where she was—then Derek's arm tightened around her waist, and everything clicked into place.

Right. His apartment. Their apartment now, technically, as of two weeks ago when she'd finally moved the last of her boxes from the house she shared with Suzie and Carlos.

She'd lived in seventeen different places over the past five years. She'd never unpacked completely in any of them, always keeping her passport accessible, her bags half-packed, her exit strategy ready.

But two weeks ago, she'd unpacked everything. Put her books on Derek's shelves (their shelves now). Hung her photos on the walls. Put her grandmother's compass on the mantle next to Derek's grandfather's watch.

She'd built roots. And they didn't feel like a trap.

"You're thinking loud," Derek mumbled into her shoulder, still half-asleep.

"How can you tell?"

"Your breathing changes when your brain is going too fast." He pressed a kiss to her shoulder blade. "What are you thinking about?"

"That I live here now. That I have an address I plan to keep for longer than six months. That's weird for me."

"Good weird or bad weird?"

"Good weird. Scary good weird." She turned in his arms to face him. His hair was sticking up in three different directions, his glasses were on the nightstand, and he looked rumpled and perfect. "How are you so calm about this?"

"About you moving in? Maya, I've been ready for this since the farmers market date. I'm just glad you finally caught up."

"I'm a slow adapter."

"You're a careful adapter. There's a difference." Derek kissed her forehead. "Coffee's ready. I set the timer last night."

"You timed the coffee maker for exactly when we'd wake up?"

"I estimated based on our average weekend wake-up time over the past three months."

"That's extremely you." But Maya was smiling. "What if we'd wanted to sleep in?"

"Then we'd have slightly cold coffee and I'd make fresh. It's not an exact science."

"Derek Chen admitting something isn't an exact science. I'm so proud of your growth."

They got up, moving around each other in the small kitchen with the ease of practice. Derek poured coffee—hers with cream, his black. Maya started breakfast—scrambled eggs, her specialty, though Derek had taught her to add a splash of milk for fluffiness.

"What's on the spontaneous adventure calendar today?" Derek asked, checking his phone.

They'd kept the system they'd developed—Derek's structured calendar with designated "spontaneity time" that Maya filled in with her current list of ideas. It was their compromise, their hybrid approach, and it worked.

"Hiking at Big Basin," Maya said. "But I was thinking we could take the scenic route, stop at that fruit stand in Los Gatos, maybe explore if we find something interesting."

"Structured spontaneity. I love it." Derek pulled up a map. "Scenic route adds thirty-five minutes but—"

"But it's worth it," Maya finished. "Because not everything has to be optimized."

"Look at you, speaking my language."

"Look at you, embracing inefficiency."

They ate breakfast on the small balcony, the October air cool but pleasant. Maya had her feet in Derek's lap, his hand absently rubbing circles on her ankle while he read something on his tablet. She was editing photos on her laptop—a new project, a book deal actually, about finding adventure in ordinary places.

Her Instagram had changed since she'd ended the Synapse experiment. Less frequent posts, more intentional content. Her follower count had dropped by about twenty percent, but her engagement was higher. Turned out people appreciated authenticity more than constant updates.

"Suzie texted," Derek said, looking at his phone. "She and James are grabbing dinner tomorrow. Elena and James, I mean. We're invited."

"How do you feel about that?"

It had been strange at first, socializing with Derek's ex-fiancée and his best friend as a couple. But six months in, it had become normal. They had dinner once a month, sometimes more. Elena and Maya had even gotten coffee a few times, just the two of them, and discovered they actually liked each other.

"I feel fine about it," Derek said. "Good, actually. Elena seems really happy."

"She is. She told me last week that she and James are thinking about moving in together."

"Fast."

"They started at 94%, remember? And they're at like 98% now. They're speed-running compatibility." Maya closed her laptop. "Do you ever wonder what our number is? Now that we're not tracking?"

"Sometimes." Derek set down his tablet. "Do you?"

"Yeah. I mean, we were at 89.7% six months ago. We've probably hit the 'exceptional long-term compatibility' threshold by now, right?"

"Maybe. Or maybe we're at 75% and just really good at working with it." Derek pulled her closer. "Does it matter?"

Maya thought about it. Six months ago, that number had meant everything. It had been permission, validation, proof. Now?

"No," she said. "It doesn't matter."

"That's growth."

"We're very growth-oriented these days."

Derek laughed, and Maya thought about how much more he laughed now. How the careful control had loosened into something more flexible. He still color-coded his calendar, still meal-prepped on Sundays, still arrived early to everything. But he also left white space, tried new restaurants without researching them first, occasionally said yes to unplanned adventures.

And Maya—Maya had a lease she'd signed without an escape clause. She had plans more than two weeks out. She'd committed to the book deal, to staying in one place long enough to finish it, to building something that required sustained effort.

They'd both changed. They were still changing. They probably always would be.

"What are you going to do about the Portland offer?" Derek asked, referencing the brand sponsorship she'd gotten last week—a month-long project that would require relocating temporarily.

"I'm going to take it," Maya said. "But I'm coming back."

"I know you are."

"How do you know?"

"Because you always come back now." Derek kissed her temple. "Also, all your stuff is here. You'd have to pack, and you hate packing."

"Rude but accurate." Maya shifted to look at him directly. "Derek, are you okay with me leaving for a month? Be honest."

"Honestly? No. I'll miss you every day. It'll mess up my routines and I'll probably call you too much and time zone math will stress me out." He smiled. "But I'm also proud of you for taking the opportunity. And I trust that you're coming back because you want to, not because you have to."

"I want to," Maya said firmly. "Portland is work. You're home."

Derek's expression did something complicated—surprise and joy and a hint of disbelief that she could mean it that completely.

"Say that again," he said.

"You're home."

"I love you."

"I love you too." She kissed him, tasting coffee and morning and certainty. "Now come on. We have a scenic route to take and spontaneous adventures to have."

"After I check the trail conditions and pack appropriate snacks."

"Obviously. I wouldn't expect anything less."

They got ready, moving around each other in the space that was theirs now. Maya caught sight of them in the bathroom mirror—her in her hiking clothes and messy ponytail, him carefully applying sunscreen with mathematical precision. They looked nothing like a "perfect match."

They looked real.

An hour later, they were in Derek's car, taking the long way to Big Basin, arguing good-naturedly about the playlist (Maya's chaotic mix versus Derek's carefully curated hiking music). They stopped at the fruit stand and bought way too many apples. They found a tiny antique shop and spent forty-five minutes browsing even though neither of them collected antiques.

"This is inefficient," Derek said, examining a vintage typewriter.

"This is fun," Maya countered. "Not everything has to be efficient."

"I know. I'm just observing." But he was smiling. "Should we get it?"

"The typewriter? What would we do with a typewriter?"

"I don't know. Display it? You could use it for your book project—writing on vintage equipment, very aesthetic."

"Derek Chen suggesting an impractical purchase for aesthetic reasons. I'm documenting this." Maya pulled out her phone.

"Don't you dare—"

She took the photo anyway—him holding the typewriter, pretending to be annoyed but clearly amused. She posted it to Instagram later that day with the caption: *Six months of teaching structure to chaos and chaos to structure. Still figuring out what we're building, but we're building it together.*

The comments were supportive, curious, warm. People who'd followed the Synapse experiment still checked in occasionally, wanting to know if they'd made it.

They had made it. They were making it. They would keep making it.

Because that was the secret the algorithm couldn't measure: love wasn't a state you achieved. It was a choice you made every day. Sometimes easy, sometimes hard, always worth it.

Derek - That Evening

They made it home from the hike as the sun was setting, both exhausted and happy and slightly sunburned despite Derek's careful sunscreen application. Maya immediately flopped on the couch, declaring she was never moving again.

Derek looked at her—at home in their space, her stuff mixed with his stuff, her books on his shelves, her chaos organized by his structure into something that somehow worked—and thought about the ring he'd bought three weeks ago.

Not yet. Not today.

But soon.

Maybe at the farmers market where he'd realized he wanted forever with her. Maybe on a spontaneous adventure she'd plan. Maybe in their living room on a random Tuesday.

He didn't need to plan it perfectly. He just needed to trust the timing.

"What are you thinking about?" Maya asked, eyes closed, clearly sensing his contemplation.

"Nothing."

"Liar. You have your 'plotting something' face."

"I'm not plotting anything."

"Yet," Maya said, opening one eye. "But you will be. Eventually. And I'm okay with that."

Derek smiled, filed that observation away, and sat beside her on the couch. She immediately curled into him, and they stayed like that as the light faded outside their windows.

Their apartment. Their life. Their choice.

71.3% or 89.7% or undefined — it didn't matter.

They were building 100% of something that was entirely theirs.

And that was more than enough.

That was everything.

[Final Instagram Post - Maya Reyes - 6 Months Post-Synapse]

People ask if the algorithm was right about us.

Turns out, it doesn't matter.

We started at 97.8% (error).
We dropped to 71.3% (correction).
We climbed to 89.7% (work).
We opted out (choice).

Six months later, we're undefined% and happy.

The algorithm introduced us. We did the rest.

To everyone who followed the #SynapseExperiment: thank you. To everyone wondering if love can be built: yes. It's hard work and daily choice and two people deciding that together is better than apart.

That's the real algorithm.

#NoMoreNumbers #JustUs #ChoosingLove

***

THE END

***